"You have a complicated life, Nina."

Jase opened the latch of the broken gate and ushered her through with a sweep of his hand.

"You have no idea, Jase."

He held his breath as she moved past him, her light fragrance tickling his nose. Would she tell him about her pregnancy? Open up about Simon?

She climbed the two porch steps and turned to face him.

He held her gaze, ready for her confidences. Not that he'd be sharing any of his own—revealing his identity was not part of his assignment—yet.

"You know that proposal you made over dinner?"

He blinked. Not what he'd been expecting, but he'd go with it. "About moving in with you? For your safety?"

"Yes. Still interested?"

"Sure."

"Good." She turned and shoved open the front door of the B and B. "Because I want you to move in—right here, right now."

THE PREGNANCY PLOT

Carol Ericson

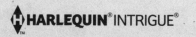
HARLEQUIN® INTRIGUE®

For the LA women (and men)
of the Los Angeles Romance Authors (LARA)

Recycling programs
for this product may
not exist in your area.

ISBN-13: 978-0-373-69851-6

The Pregnancy Plot

Copyright © 2015 by Carol Ericson

Printed in U.S.A.

Carol Ericson lives with her husband and two sons in Southern California, home of state-of-the-art cosmetic surgery, wild freeway chases and a million amazing stories. These stories, along with hordes of virile men and feisty women, clamor for release from Carol's head. It makes for some interesting headaches until she sets them free to fulfill their destinies and her readers' fantasies. To learn more about Carol, please visit her website, carolericson.com, "Where romance flirts with danger."

Books by Carol Ericson

Harlequin Intrigue

Brothers in Arms: Retribution

Under Fire
The Pregnancy Plot

Brody Law

The Bridge
The District
The Wharf
The Hill

Brothers in Arms: Fully Engaged

Run, Hide
Conceal, Protect
Trap, Secure
Catch, Release

Guardians of Coral Cove

Obsession
Eyewitness
Intuition
Deception

Visit the Author Profile page at
Harlequin.com for more titles.

CAST OF CHARACTERS

Jase Bennett—A covert ops agent who resents his assignment to babysit a pregnant woman looking for solitude, but he soon realizes his charge is in danger and he's in even greater danger of falling for her.

Nina Moore—Her ex-fiancé has dropped off the face of the earth, leaving her alone, pregnant and fearful, making it easy for her to turn to the one man who can protect her and her unborn child.

Simon Skinner—Nina's ex-fiancé has disappeared without a trace, or has he?

Lou Moore—Nina's stepsister is trouble, and her chaotic lifestyle just might threaten Nina's safety.

Kip Chandler—Lou's casual boyfriend seems befuddled by drugs and alcohol, but is his demeanor all an act?

Chris Kitchens—Simon Skinner's long-lost brother is a dead ringer for Simon; his motives for tracking down Nina seem innocent, but they might be a cover for something more sinister.

Caliban—The mysterious leader of Tempest— the black ops organization that's trying to throw world affairs into chaos—wants to rule the world and satisfy his vendetta against Jack Coburn and Prospero in the process.

Chapter One

The nurse handed her the blurry picture of her baby boy, and Nina tilted her head to the side, trying to figure out if the white, fuzzy appendage in the upper-right corner of the photo represented a foot or an arm. At just about eighteen weeks that appendage could be anything—even that which distinguished him as a boy.

The nurse smiled and flicked the edge of the ultrasound. "Well, at least if his father can't be here, you can send him his son's picture."

Nina pasted an answering smile on her face, ignoring the knife in her heart. "Yes, I'll do that."

If she could ever find her baby's father.

She hadn't wanted to get into the whole complicated story of her ex-fiancé's disappearance off the face of the earth, so she'd just told her obstetrician that her baby's father was in the military and was deployed. All good lies contained a bit of the truth.

"Make sure you stop by the front desk to make your next appointment." The nurse closed the door behind her so that Nina could get dressed.

That was another issue she hadn't discussed with her doctor yet. There wouldn't be another appointment if she decided to pull up stakes and move to Washington.

The paper crinkled as she slid off the examination

table. How had her life gotten so complicated in such a short period of time? She'd been happy with her job, happy with her fiancé and safe.

Safe? Where had that come from? She crumpled up the paper gown and shoved it into the trash can. She didn't have to dig too deeply for the answer.

She'd been feeling uneasy ever since Simon had started blowing up at the smallest issue until his ranting and raving had gotten so severe, she'd broken off their engagement over four months ago. Then he'd dropped off her radar for good. Or had he?

She squeezed into her fat jeans, making a mental note for the hundredth time that week to shop for maternity clothes.

Since her breakup with Simon, she'd had the unsettling feeling that her ex-fiancé had been stalking her—watching her, following her. She had no evidence at all to back up that suspicion, only a creeping feeling of dread. Looking over her shoulder and checking her rearview mirror had become habits for her—habits she didn't like.

Habits that gave her even more reason to leave LA for her family's bed-and-breakfast up in the Puget Sound area. The TLC that place needed since her stepfather passed away would be enough to keep her occupied.

Slipping her feet into her wedges, she hooked the strap of her purse over her shoulder. She kissed the ultrasound picture of her baby and slipped it into her purse.

She breezed into the reception area. Leaning over the counter, she said, "I need to make my next appointment."

"Of course." The receptionist's fingers raced across the keyboard of her computer. "Does this same time next month work for you, Nina?"

If the great Pacific Northwest hadn't called her home by that time. Nina peered at the calendar on the phone cupped in her hand. "Yes, and Tuesday or Wednesday of that week looks good."

"Perfect." The receptionist checked some boxes on an appointment card and held it out between two fingers.

"Thanks." Nina took the card and dropped it into her purse.

While she waited for the elevator that would take her down to the parking garage below the building, her cell phone buzzed. She glanced at the display and sighed.

Six months ago she'd been thrilled to land this job, designing the interior of a beach house in Malibu, but after Simon had gone AWOL and she'd found out she was pregnant, she had no patience for this demanding client.

She answered the call anyway. "Hello, Jennifer. Were the tiles delivered on time?"

"They arrived yesterday. I opened one of the boxes and I'm not so sure I like that yellow and blue."

Of course you don't.

The elevator doors slid open, and Nina stepped into the car, nodding at a woman holding a squirming toddler in her arms.

The woman dipped her chin while blowing a strand of hair from her face. "You need to get in your stroller now, Ben."

How did kids even move that way? He looked like a giant worm. She placed a hand on her belly. Would her baby be wiggly like that?

"Nina? I said I don't like the color."

She blinked. "If we send it back, it's going to be another two weeks, at least, before the vendor can get another shipment from Italy."

"Two weeks? I can't wait. Everything will be done by then."

"You loved the colors a month ago."

"You're right. I'll keep them."

"I'll let Fernando know the tiles are in. He and his assistant will be out tomorrow for the installation."

She ended the call at the same time the elevator stopped at the first level of the parking structure. The woman had coaxed her son into his stroller and rolled him out the door, calling over her shoulder, "Don't worry. It's all worth it."

Nina's mouth dropped open when the doors slid shut on mother and child. Had she been sending out that silent motherhood vibe?

She shifted her weight to her other foot, vowing to swap her high, wedged heels for flats any day now. She didn't need a psychiatrist to tell her that her refusal to switch up her clothes to accommodate her pregnancy was a form of denial. She absolutely wanted the baby, but the pregnancy had been a surprise, and coming on the heels of her breakup with Simon, it had been an overwhelming surprise.

But one she could handle, one she couldn't wait to handle.

The doors swooshed open on her parking level and she got a whiff of exhaust fumes. She waved her hand in front of her face. She'd definitely be breathing cleaner air if she made the move from LA to Washington, but she'd be leaving her life and her friends behind.

As she headed for her car in the far corner of the parking lot, her cell buzzed again. She held her phone up to her face in the dim light of the garage and squinted at a text from Jennifer—more doubts about the yellow tile.

Pinning her purse to her body with the inside of her elbow, she used both thumbs to text Jennifer some more encouragement. She sent the text and looked up.

"Three C?" she said to herself. She'd missed her aisle.

As she backtracked, a slow-moving car on the row above caught her attention. Unlike when she'd arrived for her appointment this afternoon, the parking garage sported plenty of empty slots. No need for that car to be rolling along at such a slow speed past vacant parking spaces.

In contrast to the speed of the car, her heart rate ticked up a few notches. She turned down the aisle where she'd parked her car and moved as fast as her shoes would allow.

Holding her key fob in front of her, she clicked it over and over just to make sure the car would be unlocked when she reached it.

She glanced over her shoulder at the other car, a black sedan, now crawling down the ramp to her level. She slid out of her shoes, grabbed them with one hand and jogged toward her car.

A woman getting into her car turned to stare at her. Nina didn't care what she looked like running to her car.

She grabbed the handle, pulled open the door and dropped onto the seat, smashing her fist against the automatic lock. The woman who'd been eyeballing her started her own car and pulled out, giving Nina full view of the end of the row.

The slow-moving sedan showed up in the aisle, and Nina cranked on her ignition. If that car decided to follow her, she'd drive straight to a police station. If the driver was Simon, he'd get the picture soon enough that, baby or no baby, she'd press charges against him for stalking if he kept up this cloak-and-dagger stuff. All he had to do was call her.

Her car's ignition clicked, but the car didn't start. She tried again, clenching her teeth against the grating sound coming from her car. She didn't need car trouble now.

She cut off the unresponsive engine, took a deep breath and turned the key one more time. Again, the engine failed to turn over.

The black car had turned around on the next level and

was heading back toward her again. A cold fear seized her. She didn't know if it was Simon or someone else in that car with the tinted windows, but she sensed a powerful evil heading in her direction.

She cupped her hands over her barely discernible belly, and a surge of protectiveness rushed through her body. She removed her key from the ignition and pressed the red panic button on the remote.

Her car alarm blared alternately with her honking horn as she slid down in her seat.

With her nose just above the steering wheel, she watched the car zoom past her.

A minute later, a man and a woman were knocking on her car window.

She buzzed down the window, and the woman poked her head inside the car. "Are you okay?"

Nina's heart slowed its gallop. "I'm fine. I…I was trying to start my car, and I hit the alarm on my remote by mistake."

No point in revealing her emotional instability to anyone else. That's all it was—pregnancy hormones running amok.

The woman stepped back. "We saw you slip down in your seat and thought you were having some kind of medical emergency."

"No. I'm fine."

The man shrugged and turned away, obviously less interested than the woman, concern still creasing her face.

"Can you start your car now?"

Nina turned the key and got the same noise. "I guess not."

"Can you get a ride?"

The man glanced at his watch.

"I have an automobile club service. I'll call them." Nina popped her door handle, since she had no intention of waiting for the tow truck in this rapidly clearing parking lot.

The woman smiled. "You take care now."

Nina slung her purse over her shoulder and trudged back to the elevator, periodically glancing over her shoulder to look out for the black sedan.

Was it just a coincidence that her car broke down at the very same time a mysterious vehicle seemed to be shadowing her in the parking structure?

Maybe, maybe not, but the scare had just sealed her fate.

She was leaving LA for Break Island, Washington, sooner rather than later.

JASE FLIPPED UP the collar of his jacket and shoved his hands into his pockets, as the ferry chugged into port. Who the hell would leave sunny Southern California for this godforsaken island in the middle of Puget Sound at this time of the year?

Crazy pregnant lady.

When Jase reached land, he ordered a cup of coffee from the window next to the ticket office. He balanced the cup on the edge of a planter and pulled out his phone.

Jack Coburn picked up on the first ring.

"Jack, I made it to Break Island. I have no idea why anyone would want to open a bed-and-breakfast on this rock. No wonder the place closed down."

Coburn cleared his throat. "Fishing, sailing, hiking, bird-watching at the sanctuary, and ferries to Vancouver and Seattle. The Moonstones B&B didn't close down for lack of business. Nina Moore's mother became ill and passed away. After her mother's death, her stepfather committed suicide."

Coburn always did his homework. Jase had known all that about Nina Moore's tragic history, but he'd been too busy arguing with Coburn about this babysitting job to really take note of her background. Sad stuff—and she didn't even know about her ex-fiancé yet.

Coburn read his thoughts. "You would've remembered all that if you hadn't been so intent on protesting the assignment. I need you focused, Bennett."

"I'm on it, boss. Protect the pregnant lady."

"We have to cover all our bases. We don't know what's going on right now or what to believe from Max Duvall's crazy stories."

"The body of Nina Moore's fiancé hasn't turned up yet, has it?"

"Nope."

"Maybe he's not even dead."

"Maybe not, but that doesn't change our mission."

"Protect the pregnant lady."

"Exactly."

Jase ended the call and squinted through the gray haze that enveloped the small town rolling out in front of him. Maybe the pregnant lady had escaped to Break Island to hide her condition from her ex-fiancé. He snorted and snatched his coffee from the planter.

Wouldn't be the first time a woman had tried to hide a pregnancy from a man.

He checked into a small motel in the center of town and returned to the office to get to work. He touched the bell on the counter, and the motel's proprietor came out from the back.

"Everything okay in your room?"

"Everything's fine." He picked up a flyer about the island's bird sanctuary and tucked it into his pocket. "Maisie, right?"

"That's right."

In true small-town fashion, Maisie had introduced herself when he checked in. "On my way in on the ferry, I noticed a B and B on the shore. It looked kind of rough but still open. Any chance the owner needs some help fixing up the place? I'm looking for a little work, and that's right up my alley."

"I don't know if Nina's looking for help, but she should be. Moonstones has been empty for a few years now and could sure use some TLC."

"Thanks, Maisie." He rapped his knuckles on the counter. "I think I'll head over there and see if I can offer Nina some TLC."

Once outside, Jase adjusted his shoulder holster beneath his blue flannel shirt. He'd fit right in with these lumberjack types.

He jogged down the steps of the motel, which sat at the end of the main street, and headed for the path that led down to the beach. He made a left turn, hugging the shoreline as he scuffed along the sandy path toward Nina's B and B. Moonstones perched on a rocky beach on the far edge of town, along with a few other beach houses. Nina must've really wanted to get away from it all.

He traipsed through the sand and clambered over some rocks to get a good view of the building before approaching it.

A tangled garden spilled over the ramshackle fence that ringed the property. One blue shutter hung by a broken hinge, revealing a crack in the window. This didn't look like a prime spot for someone expecting a baby.

But Coburn had ordered him to get close to the subject, and this ramshackle B and B offered the perfect opportunity. He wouldn't be his grandfather's disciple if he didn't know his way around a hammer and nail—even though Dad had disapproved.

He shuffled through the dry sand and crossed the road to the B and B. The battered wooden gate sagged and he pushed through to the garden in the front. Using the rusty hook, he latched the gate behind him.

This place wouldn't provide much security if someone wanted to get to Nina. He had to make sure that didn't happen.

He veered off the overgrown walkway to the front of the B and B, slogging through the knee-high weeds, and cut a path to the corner of the building. He peered around it, taking in a deck with patio furniture stacked in the corner and a fire pit crisscrossed with charred logs.

Squinting, he could almost envision a circle of guests around a roaring fire, toasting marshmallows as the waves lapped at the dock where the boats gently bobbed. Almost.

He hooked his thumb in the front pocket of his jeans and started to turn back…but the unmistakable sound of a shotgun being readied for use stopped him in his tracks.

Chapter Two

His adrenaline pulsed for two beats, as his finger twitched for his weapon. Then he took a deep breath. If one of his enemies had a gun on him, he'd already be dead.

A woman's voice barked out an order. "Put your hands in the air and turn around...slowly."

He complied and added a smile to his face for good measure.

Nina Moore held him at bay with an old shotgun that looked as if it had seen its best days during the Civil War. Her dark ponytail hung over one shoulder and she widened her stance as she leveled the barrel of the shotgun right between his eyes.

Crazy pregnant lady.

"Who the hell are you and what are you doing on my property?"

"My name's Jase Buckley and I heard you needed some help fixing up this place."

Her eyes narrowed. He couldn't quite catch their color from here, but they glittered dangerously.

"Who told you that?"

"Maisie—the woman at my motel." He'd led Maisie on, but she would at least verify that they'd had a conversation about how the owner of Moonstones might need help repairing the place. "I'm new on the island. I came here to do some writing, but I also need to earn some cash."

"Maisie, huh?" The gun slipped a little and she tapped the toe of her sneaker on the sandy ground. "I can check out your story."

"Go right ahead." He waved his hands in the air. "Can I put my arms down now?"

She loosened her grip on the shotgun and pinned it against her side. "I *could* use some help around here, but I fully intend to check you out."

"I thought Break Island was one of those friendly, small-town places." He cocked his head. "Didn't realize you could get shot going up to someone's front door."

"You didn't go up to my front door." She tipped her chin toward him. "You came around here to the side."

He jerked his thumb over his shoulder. "I was admiring the deck and the fire pit, or at least admiring what it could be."

She ran her tongue along her lower lip, her shoulders still rigid. "Yeah, I plan to fix that up…eventually."

He hadn't expected Nina to be on edge, unless she always greeted strangers with a shotgun. Had someone attempted to contact her already? What did she know about her ex-fiancé's disappearance?

"I can help you with that." He cleared his throat as his gaze swept across her lean frame, no baby bump in sight. He'd have to pretend he knew nothing of her pregnancy. "I'll be on the island for a while, and I need some gainful employment."

"What do you write?"

Shoving his hands into his pockets, he kicked at a rock on the crumbling path. "I'm a former marine, did a few tours in Afghanistan. Thought I'd write what I know, a fictional account."

Her eyes widened and her fingers curled around the butt of the shotgun. "Y-you're military?"

"Retired." He thought it best to stick as close to the

truth as possible, but his military background bothered her—must be memories of her ex-fiancé, Simon Skinner. She *had* ended it with Skinner before he disappeared. Maybe they'd had a bad breakup.

With his hands still stuffed in his pockets, he lifted his shoulders to his ears. "Just thought I had an interesting story to tell, but the book's not a bestseller yet. Hell, the book isn't even written yet. That's why I need to make some money while I figure out if this story will write itself."

"I do have a soft spot for military men." She blinked and rested one hand on her stomach. "My...my stepfather was in the navy."

And her ex-fiancé was a navy SEAL before joining Tempest as an agent...and winding up dead.

"I hope you'll give this vet a chance." He swept his arm across her property. "I can help you out here."

She puffed a breath of air from between her lips as if she'd been holding it. "Maybe. Give me a day or two to check you out, and a couple of references wouldn't hurt. Can't pay you much more than minimum wage."

"I'll get right on the references. Thanks." He pointed to the purse she'd dropped on the ground next to her before leveling the gun at his head. "Were you going out?"

"I'm going across the bay to the mainland to pick up some supplies."

"Can I help you?"

"No." She picked up the gun in her hands again and made a move toward the house.

She hadn't been joking about looking into his background first. A woman in her condition should be cautious and he was glad Nina was, unlike some women he knew, but she'd obviously brought her big-city paranoia to the small town.

As she retreated to the house, he scuffed through the

sand toward the front gate and left it open behind him. He clambered on top of a pile of rocks and faced the bay, his eyes watering at the sharp, cold breeze stinging his face.

He hadn't brought the full Bennett charm into play yet—just didn't seem right with a pregnant woman, even though he wasn't supposed to know she was expecting—but it looked as if it was going to be harder than he'd imagined getting close to Nina Moore.

And for some strange reason, he'd completely changed his mind about this assignment after meeting his quarry. He couldn't wait to get close to Nina Moore.

NINA LOCKED THE front door behind her and cursed the weeds as she slogged through them to the sagging gate. Her pulse jumped as she spied Jase on the rocks in front of the property next door. Was he waiting for her?

She'd felt such a connection to him the moment he'd turned and faced her shotgun. He had a quality that reminded her of Simon—not his looks. Simon was a good-looking guy, too, but his red hair and broad features were worlds apart from Jase's dark intensity. Both men had an air of watchful readiness about them, as if they could spring into action at any moment.

They also both shared a commanding presence, giving her the uneasy feeling that she'd do their bidding even at her own peril. All a man had to do was promise to lead and she'd follow him anywhere.

Must be the pregnancy hormones making her crazy. She shook her head and tossed her ponytail over her shoulder.

She latched the gate and veered left. Her sneakers hit the wood planks leading to the boat dock where Dad's sixteen-foot boat bobbed in the water. Keeping one eye on Jase still peering at the bay, she started the seventy-horsepower engine. It sputtered and coughed and then rumbled to life. She aimed the boat toward the line of shore she could just make out in the distance.

The salty breeze whipped the ponytail across her face, and she stuck out her tongue to catch the spray just because she felt like it. She glanced over her shoulder at Jase, still on the rocks, his figure getting smaller and smaller although he still loomed large in her mind.

It must be that inner spit and polish that gave military men their bearing, leaving the impression of invincibility. That's why Simon's behavior had been so frightening. At first she'd pegged it as post-traumatic stress disorder and had encouraged him to visit a therapist, but he'd have none of that. The same personality traits that gave him supreme control in the face of danger also led him to an impenetrable stubbornness.

She sighed and slightly shifted the course of the boat. If Simon ever wanted to be part of his son's life, he'd have to get some counseling first.

She shivered and stamped her feet—in a puddle. She looked down, gasping at the pool of water sloshing over her sneakers. The spray hadn't been that high or wild to flood the boat—not yet anyway, although a storm was on its way down from Alaska.

She skimmed the toe of her wet shoe across the bottom of the boat and more water gushed in. Bending over, she ran her fingers across the fiberglass surface, her tips tripping over the edge of some electrical tape.

"Are you kidding me?" She peeled back the tape, exposing a hole in the fiberglass the size of a quarter and getting bigger as more water gurgled into the boat.

She rose, jerking her head toward the mainland and then toward the island. Faster to go back.

She eased into a turn and started chugging back to Break Island. The boat lurched and listed as it took on more water the faster she went. When the water got ankle-high, she slowed the boat and tried to bail out with a bucket.

When the left stern started to dip, she abandoned the idea of a bailout and eyed the shoreline of the island. Even if she could swim that distance with her clothes dragging her down, the water would be freezing cold. Would her baby feel the cold?

How had this happened? She kicked the side of the boat. When she'd checked out the boat a few days ago, she thought she'd found one thing at Moonstones that still worked.

The boat limped several more yards toward Break Island, and Nina climbed onto the seat cushions and waved her arms above her head. Did she even have a beacon on this thing?

In the distance, across the water, two boats seemed to be charging hard toward her. One had come straight from the boat docks on her side of the island and the other had rounded the bend from the town side of the island. Had they actually seen her or were they just out for a boat ride across the bay?

She flapped her arms to her sides like a giant bird and jumped—bad idea. The water in the belly of the boat sloshed and the outboard motor swung to one side, lifting the other side of the boat out of the water.

She stepped off the seat and shuffled to the leeward side of the boat. A loud crack resounded and the whooshing sound of water pushing through a small opening had her grabbing the bin where Dad had stored life jackets.

Why hadn't she thought of that before? Gripping the edge of the lid, she paused, lifting her head to check on the progress of those two boats. The one from the docks by the B and B was still making a beeline toward her, while the other seemed to have disappeared. Maybe that one never saw her.

She grabbed an orange life jacket and slipped it over her head. She knew how to swim, but the flotation device would keep her afloat until her cavalry came to the rescue in case the cold water made her cramp up or her heavy clothes dragged her down into the murky water of the sound.

The boat rocked and she planted her feet on the deck beneath the water to steady herself, but the little fiberglass boat couldn't take it. One side of the boat went under and the force flung her into the icy embrace of the bay.

The cold sucked the air from her lungs for a moment, paralyzing her, and then she made a grab for the side of the capsized boat. Her hands clawed against the slippery fiberglass until she found a hold.

The hum of an outboard motor got louder and louder, and she would've yelled out to make sure the boat was going to stop but her teeth were chattering so much she couldn't get a sound past her lips.

She didn't need to. The other boat's motor cut out as it drew next to her incapacitated vessel. It floated around to her side, and a strong hand reached for her.

"Oh, my God. Are you all right, Nina?"

Tossing wet strands of hair back from her face, she looked into the dark eyes of Jase Buckley—her savior, or was he?

Chapter Three

His grip tightened around her wrists. "Are you ready? I'm going to haul you up."

With her teeth chattering, she nodded and braced her feet against the side of the boat.

Jase lifted her into the boat with ease, despite the eight extra pounds she'd packed on during her pregnancy. She glanced over her shoulder at her boat, now heavy with water, and shivered. She could've clung to the side, but she might've been there awhile if Jase and that other boat hadn't been on the sound.

"What the hell happened?" Jase shrugged out of his flannel shirt, draped it over her shoulders and tucked it around her body.

"There was a hole in the bottom and it started taking on water."

"Should we try to tow it back in?" He crouched next to a bin on the deck of the boat and tugged at the padlock securing the lid.

"I'll call the Harbor Patrol when we get back to shore. They patrol the sound and they'll bring it in for me."

"If it hasn't sunk to the bottom of the sound by then."

She hunched her shoulders against the chill snaking through her body. "It's insured if it does. Do you think we can get my purse off the boat? It's hooked onto the side."

"I'll try." He brought his boat abreast of hers, planted one foot on the ailing boat and snagged the purse. "Got it."

Safely back in her neighbors' boat, he handed the purse to her. "When was the last time you took that thing out on the water?"

"It's been a few years. I haven't been in it since I've been back. I meant to give it the once-over, but there were just so many other things to do."

"That's because you need some help." He aimed the boat toward the shoreline.

Narrowing her eyes, she sniffed through what was probably a very red nose right now. What better way to get her to trust him than by staging a rescue? How long had Jase been snooping around the B and B and her boat dock before she'd discovered him in her yard?

"You look like you're freezing."

The wind raked its fingers through Jase's chocolate-brown hair and infused his face with a ruddy glow. No pinched, red nose for him. He looked like an advertisement for some brisk aftershave.

"I am freezing. This water is not meant for a leisurely dip, especially with that storm from Alaska on its way." She rubbed the back of her hand across her nose and pressed a palm against the small rise in her belly. Hopefully, the baby was still snug and cozy.

Jase's eyes dropped to the movement and then shifted to stare at the land rushing toward them.

"Hang on. Not too much longer."

"You borrowed this boat from the Kleinschmidts next door."

"I figured they wouldn't mind if I used it in the commission of a rescue."

There it was again—pumping himself up as her savior. She crossed her arms, cupping her elbows and blowing out a long breath. She needed to relax. He *was* her savior.

Why would Simon send someone out here to do his bidding for him and why would a man like this be interested in doing that bidding?

"You're my savior because you got here faster than the other guy."

"The other guy?" His brow crinkled as he nudged the rudder.

"Another boat was headed my way from the other side of the peninsula, the town side. I think he must've turned around when he saw you had the situation covered."

"Really?" He downshifted and the boat chugged to a choppy crawl. "You'd think he would've come out anyway to make sure everything was okay."

"Maybe he didn't see me at all and continued across the sound."

"Maybe." He steered the boat back into the Kleinschmidts' dock. "Can you reach the county patrol now?"

"Probably." She dug into her bag and pulled out her phone.

Jase expertly maneuvered the boat into the dock and held out his hand to help her onto dry land. "You make that call while I secure the boat."

Turning her back to him, she placed the call, and ten minutes later, just as Jase hopped onto the wooden dock, Nina spied the red county patrol boat heading toward her disabled craft.

"Do they need you to tow that back here?"

"No. They'll secure it to my dock."

"Good." He squeezed her shoulders, still trembling beneath the blue flannel of his damp shirt. "Let's get you inside and get you something hot to drink. Coffee?"

"I don't drink coffee—anymore."

"And I only drink it first thing in the morning. Do you have some tea or hot chocolate?"

"I have some chamomile tea, if you like."

"It's not for me. It's for you." He spun her around and marched behind her, his hands lightly on the back of her shoulders.

"You're the one missing a shirt. That white T-shirt isn't enough to protect you against the harsh elements out here." Although she hadn't minded the way the thin cotton had molded to his muscles. Simon had been broader and beefier than this man with his lean muscles and patrician features. But Jase didn't come off any less capable than Simon. In fact, they both possessed a similar air of efficiency and confidence—that is until Simon changed.

Strong fingers dug into the sides of her neck. "You okay? Your back is as stiff as a board."

"Just cold." She traipsed up the two steps of the porch, escaping his touch, and fumbled for her keys. She shouldn't be getting that much pleasure out of Jase's warm touch while carrying Simon's baby.

Not that she would ever trust Simon in their child's life—at least not until he got some help for his anger issues.

What the hell had he been so angry about anyway?

The keys dropped from her shaking hands, and Jase scooped them up in one fluid movement. "Let me."

He slid the key home and pushed open the door, stepping to the side.

She ducked around him, the condition of the B and B bringing warmth to her cold cheeks. She really hadn't made much progress. It didn't help that every afternoon a slow, sneaking lethargy stole over her body.

She waved at the sitting room with its worn wood floors and blackened fireplace. "I still have a lot of work to do."

"That's what I'd heard. You change into some dry clothes." He dangled the keys from one finger. "And I'll boil some water for tea."

Snatching the keys from him, she pivoted away from him. And just like that she'd allowed another controlling male into her life.

She called over her shoulder, "Tea bags are in the cupboard to the left of the stove."

"I can handle it. Get those wet clothes off and change into something comfortable."

Nina turned, sucked in her lower lip and studied Jase's handsome face. He seemed a little too interested in getting her out of her clothes.

She dipped her head once and said, "I still have that shotgun."

His eyes widened above raised hands. "Yes, ma'am."

Tossing a strand of wet hair over her shoulder, she crossed to her separate living quarters tucked behind the staircase. She'd make it quick and get out of this flannel shirt that had Jase's fresh, manly scent in every fold.

She didn't need any more complications in her life right now.

WHEN HE HEARD a door close in the back of the house, Jase whistled through his teeth and turned toward the kitchen. That woman had a suspicious mind. Maybe it came from being pregnant…or dating a spy. A spy who had disappeared. That would do it.

A copper teapot perched on a burner, and he grabbed it by the handle and filled it with water from the tap. A couple of mugs dangled from a wooden tree. He plucked them off, reading the words printed on the white one aloud, "Number one runner."

He figured Nina for the runner, since she looked like someone in good shape, despite the pregnancy, not that a woman couldn't be pregnant and in good shape, but he hoped she wasn't out there running marathons. He banged one of the mugs on the counter with a little too much force. Hell, what did he know?

He claimed the plain, red mug with the chip on the handle for himself. Then he swung open the cupboard to the left of the range and took out the box of chamomile tea. He'd rather have a snifter of cognac to warm up, but he didn't figure Nina would have any booze on hand.

By the time the kettle whistled, Nina had returned, wedging a shoulder against the refrigerator, hugging a shapeless, red sweater around her body.

She wrinkled her nose. "You don't look too comfortable in the kitchen."

"Really?" He swung a tea bag in the air, wrapping the string around his finger. "I thought I was doing a bang-up job in here."

"Find everything okay?" She had scooped her shoulder-length, dark hair back into its ponytail, and the tilt of her head sent it swinging behind her.

"I did." He held up the runner's mug. "Is this you?"

Shoving her hands into the pockets of her jeans, she lifted her shoulder to her ears. "I ran cross-country in college."

"Impressive. Here in Washington?"

"Oregon."

"A runner's paradise—even more impressive." He poured the bubbling water over the tea bags in the cups, and the rising steam gave a much-needed homey touch to the dilapidated kitchen.

She joined him at the counter to take her mug, her shoulder brushing against his, the fuzzy softness of her sweater tickling his arm through his T-shirt. Her pale, stiff fingers curled around the handle of the mug.

What she really needed was a warm bath, but if he suggested that, she'd probably haul out that shotgun again.

"Does that fireplace in the other room work?"

"Yes, and I even have a cord of wood that my neighbor delivered—the same neighbor who owns that boat you borrowed." She tapped his mug with her fingernail. "Do you want some sugar or milk for that?"

Since he never drank tea, he didn't have a clue. "I, uh, take it black."

She wrapped her hands around the cup, closed her eyes and sniffed the steam floating up from the mug. Her long lashes created dark crescents on her cheeks, and her full lips curved into a slight smile.

He caught his breath at the simple beauty of her expression and then shook his head. Put him in the presence of a pregnant woman and his thoughts went haywire. Nina wasn't Maggie, and the baby she was carrying was Simon Skinner's, not his.

"Let's get this fire started." And he didn't mean the one that had been doing a slow burn in his belly ever since he locked his gaze onto Nina Moore.

She skirted past him, her pale cheeks sporting two red spots, as if she could read his mind.

He followed her into the great room, which must've functioned as a sitting room and gathering place for guests—when there were guests.

She gestured toward the big stone fireplace that took up half the wall. "I've already used it once, so I know it works, unlike the boat."

"Speaking of the boat." He swept aside the curtain at the front window and peered outside. "Looks like they're bringing it in, so at least they saved it from sinking."

"I'll look at it later." Nina collapsed into a recliner, facing the fireplace and folding her hands around her cup.

She looked as if she needed warming up, and even though he had a few impure thoughts about how he could do that, he placed his mug on the table beside her and crouched in front of the fireplace and got to work.

"Did I ever say thank you?"

"For?" He cupped his hand around the orange flicker as it raced across the edge of the newspaper crumpled beneath the logs.

"For rescuing me out there on the bay. Even though I wasn't in imminent danger of drowning, the water was freezing cold and…"

He held his breath. Would she mention her pregnancy now?

She coughed. "And I could've been floating out there for a while before another boat came along."

He let out his breath and prodded a log into place before rising to his feet and retrieving his tasteless tea.

He eased into a love seat at right angles to Nina's chair and the fire, crackling to life. "There was that other boat. They were probably on their way to save you when they saw me. I'm glad I could get to you faster."

She stretched her long legs in front of her, crossing her legs at the ankles. She'd gotten rid of her sodden sneakers, her feet now encased in a pair of soft red socks that matched her sweater. Her coloring played well against the red, her blue eyes a contrast to her dark hair, giving her an exotic look.

Simon Skinner had been a redhead. The baby could be an interesting combination of Mom and Dad.

Then the truth punched him in the gut. If her ex-fiancé and the father of her baby was dead, she had a right to know. They had only Max Duvall's word for that now, but once they received confirmation, he'd convince Jack Coburn that they had to tell Nina.

He didn't like it when people kept the truth from him, and he wouldn't be a party to doing that to someone else.

Of course, he was in the wrong line of work for those sentiments.

The fire danced higher, creating a wall of warmth, and Nina held her hands out toward it, wiggling her fingers.

"Are you warming up?"

"Slowly but surely." She pointed to his cup, still brimming with pale gold liquid. "You're not drinking your tea."

"I'm not the one who wound up treading water in the sound for ten minutes."

"True, but you did give up your flannel and had to cross the bay in nothing but a flimsy T-shirt." Her gaze flicked over his chest, and he resisted the urge to flex.

That glance alone did more to heat him up than ten cups of chamomile could.

She snapped her fingers as if to break the spell between them. "I hung up your shirt in the bathroom, but maybe it would dry faster in front of this fire."

She scooted forward on her chair and he held up his hand. "I'll get it. Tell me where."

"Down the hall past the staircase, through the door and the bathroom's the first room on your right. Those quarters are separate from the rest of the B and B."

He pushed up from the chair, taking his cup with him. He made a detour to the kitchen and placed it in the sink.

Nina called from the other room. "You could've asked for something stronger."

"I hate drinking alone."

She turned in her seat as he came out of the kitchen and she cocked her head. "How'd you know I wouldn't join you? You didn't ask."

"You seemed hell-bent on tea." He shrugged and ducked behind the staircase.

Idiot. He planted the heel of his hand against his forehead. If his boss could see the way he was conducting this assignment, Coburn would pull his secret agent card.

He pushed open the door to the small bathroom and snagged his shirt from the shower curtain rod.

His hand hovered at the corner of the medicine cabinet and then he abruptly turned and exited the bathroom. He was here to watch over Nina, not spy on her.

His agency didn't suspect her of any wrongdoing and she deserved her privacy.

He shook out the still-damp shirt in front of him as he returned to the great room. After he'd boarded the boat to go after Nina, he suspected he might have to go into the water after her, so he'd stashed his weapon and shoulder holster on the neighbors' boat. He hoped they didn't decide to take it out for a spin.

The fire was in its full glory, and the glow from the flames cast an aura over Nina, backlighting her dark hair as she turned toward him and giving her face a rosy sheen.

"Is it still wet?"

"A little." He dragged an ottoman in front of the fireplace and spread his shirt on top of it. "This should do the trick."

He sprawled in his chair, wedging his ankle on the opposite knee. "So what made you come out here and open a B and B?"

"I grew up here, and it seemed like a good idea to come home and try to get this place back into shape. My mom and stepdad ran it until…their health failed. That's why it's just a mess now."

"Sorry." He opened his mouth to say more, but a horn from a boat bellowed outside. "What is that? Sounds like an angry moose."

"That—" she struggled to her feet from the deep chair "—is the county rescue boat. They must be pulling my craft into the dock."

Jase snatched his warm shirt from the ottoman and stuffed his arms into the sleeves. "I'll go have a look."

"I'll join you. It's my boat." She slipped her feet into

a pair of clogs and grabbed a hoodie from a hook by the front door.

Sure enough, the big red Harbor Patrol boat had backed Nina's damaged craft against her dock.

They approached a member of the rescue team who was leaning over the side of the boat and writing something on a clipboard.

"Afternoon, folks. This your boat?"

"It's mine." Nina waved her hand. "I made the call."

"You must be Bruce and Lori's girl."

"That's right. I'm Nina Moore."

"Well, Nina Moore. I'm afraid I have some bad news for you."

Jase instinctively stepped in front of Nina. "What's the bad news?"

"This hole here?" The man jerked his thumb over his shoulder. "Someone did that on purpose."

Chapter Four

Jack Coburn had been right about this assignment and the need to watch over Skinner's ex-fianceé. Someone had Nina in his crosshairs already.

Two vertical lines formed between Nina's eyebrows, and she kicked the toe of her clog against a wooden post. "I figured it was just a matter of time."

He jerked his head up. Nina knew about Tempest?

The patrol officer tipped his hat back. "You have an idea who did this, Ms. Moore?"

"You can call me Nina, and yes. It has to be my stepsister, Lou." She swept her arm across the bay as if the mysterious Lou lurked somewhere out there on the water.

"Oh, yeah, Lou." The officer nodded in a way that made Jase feel completely out of the loop. "I remember her. Do you have any proof she did this?"

"None at all, except that someone in town mentioned they'd seen her around. So, she's back on the island."

"Watch your back, Ms.—Nina." The officer smacked the side of Nina's boat and jumped onto his own.

Jase watched the Harbor Patrol boat for a minute as it maneuvered away from the dock, and then turned to Nina. "Why would your stepsister be putting holes in your boat?"

Keeping her gaze on the retreating patrol boat, she

crossed her arms over her waist and her sweater outlined a small bump below, the first visible sign of her pregnancy— at least to him. Nina's lean runner's frame would probably take a while to show evidence of her condition, but she had to be at least four or five months along, judging by the last time she saw Skinner.

He'd seen pictures of Maggie pregnant at about the same stage as Nina, and she'd had a distinctive rounded belly, but then Maggie was smaller and more rounded in general than Nina.

When Nina swung her head around, his gaze jumped to her face.

"My stepsister, Lou, is a disturbed person. She's had some problems with drugs and alcohol, but her issues go beyond that. When her father married my mother and Mom and I came to live with them when she and I were both children, she had a fit. It only got worse from there. I knew when Dad, Bruce, left this B and B to me, she'd never let it go."

"So, you think she's bent on sabotage?" Noticing a tremble rolling through her body, he took Nina's arm. "Let's go back inside. You're still chilled from your swim in the sound."

She allowed him to steer her back toward the house. "Putting a hole in the bottom of my boat would definitely be something in Lou's repertoire."

"Is she capable of more? Would she do you physical harm? Not that plunging into the icy depths of that bay couldn't have resulted in something worse than a bad chill."

Pushing open the door, she paused on the threshold. "I don't think she'd pull out a gun and shoot me, but she'd pull stunts that could have unintended consequences— just like putting a hole in a boat."

"And I thought my family had issues." He stomped his feet on the mat at the door.

"Oh?"

He had no intention of getting personal with her and mentally gave himself a kick for even mentioning his family. He'd used his nickname and a fake last name, just in case she decided to do a little research on the internet, because it wouldn't be hard to find Jason Bennett—or his family.

"Do you want more tea?" He pointed to the flames simmering in the grate. "Looks like the fire died down."

"I'm fine." She stood in the entryway, making no move to go back to their cozy situation in front of the fire.

"Okay, I'll be heading back to my motel. Do you want me to stoke that up for you before I go?" He made a move toward the fireplace, but she placed a hand on his arm.

"I'll let it go, thanks."

He strode past her anyway. "I'll reposition those logs, so they don't roll off the grate."

He couldn't help it. Nina's pregnancy gave him an overwhelming urge to do things for her—all the things he never got to do for Maggie. He prodded the logs and then snagged Nina's mug and deposited it in the kitchen sink next to his.

Shoving his hands into his pockets, he grinned because women had told him in the past he had an irresistible grin and he needed to be irresistible right now. "Let me know when you're done checking me out and I can get to work for you around here."

"Oh, I'm done. Anyone who rescues me from drowning deserves a chance." She sized him up beneath lowered lashes. "You can start tomorrow."

"Awesome." He stuck out his hand and she gripped it. "I'll be back around eight o'clock."

Her blue eyes widened. "Make it ten."

"You got it…boss."

When he reached the curve in the road that led back to the town, he pulled his cell phone from his pocket and called Coburn.

"What do you have for me, Jase?"

"I met Nina Moore and she hired me as her handyman. I start tomorrow."

Coburn chuckled. "Must be that killer grin of yours. Is she suspicious about anything? Did she mention the father of her baby?"

"The father?" Jase glanced over his shoulder at the empty road. "She didn't even mention the baby. She's, uh, not really showing, so the subject never came up."

"She's gotta be five months along and she's not showing?"

"Yeah, your wife had twins, so I think that's a different case."

"Probably. What do I know anyway?" Coburn coughed. "You okay with this assignment?"

Jase chose to ignore Coburn's implication. Jack made it his business to know the personal histories of all Prospero agents, and sometimes Jase thought he used those histories just to test them, to mess with their minds.

"I'm never okay with babysitting assignments, Coburn, but you might be onto something here."

His boss sucked in a breath. "Oh, yeah?"

"Someone drilled a hole in Nina's boat and she discovered it while she was on the water."

"Is she okay?"

"Chilled but fine."

"You think it might be our friends at Tempest?"

"If they're trying to kill her, sinking her boat on a well-traveled bay is a long shot. Seems Nina has some crazy family members in the mix, too."

"Great. Just keep doing your job, Jase—watch Nina Moore and protect her if necessary."

"Got it, boss."

Jase ended the call and tapped the phone against his chin. He'd have no problem either watching or protecting Nina Moore. He'd do whatever it took to safeguard Nina and the baby—Simon Skinner's baby.

NINA STRIPPED OFF her clothes and turned sideways in front of the mirror as the bathtub filled with warm water. She massaged her bump with the palm of her hand and smiled. Her little guy was growing by leaps and bounds.

Had Jase noticed her pregnancy? No way. Any hint of a pregnancy would've doused those scorching looks he'd been sending her all afternoon. She'd been enjoying those looks so much she hadn't wanted them to end.

What did that say about her? Carrying another man's baby and getting hot and bothered by a stranger with a to-die-for grin. Simon had vanished from her life, but it didn't mean he didn't plan on charging back into it.

And she needed to be prepared when he did.

She stood on her tiptoes and checked the lock on the bathroom window. When the Harbor Patrol officer had told her about the hole in the boat, her suspicions had immediately turned to Lou, since any mischief connected to the B and B would have Lou written all over it.

But had Simon followed her here? He knew about the B and B, of course, even though he'd never been here. She rolled her shoulders and stepped into the warm water, inhaling the fragrant steam from the lilac bath salts.

She'd found a good doctor in town, a family practitioner rather than an ob-gyn, but Dr. Parducci had come highly rated and regarded.

She sank into the warm water, stretched out her legs

and closed her eyes, determined to relax. Dr. Parducci had told her to relax and not dwell on anything stressful.

Her eyes flew open. Like Lou. That had been the most unwelcome piece of news when she'd returned to Break Island. Had Lou known she was coming back to claim the B and B? Lou had no interest in the place, but she'd been livid when Bruce had left it to his stepdaughter instead of his daughter.

What did she expect? Her father had loved this place. Turning it over to Lou would've resulted in a quick sale and money blown on drugs, booze and a good time.

Nina closed her eyes again and swirled her hands in the silky water, willing her mind to happier thoughts.

Jase Buckley—now, there was a happy thought. Something about that man attracted her like a magnet. It could be his general drop-dead gorgeousness. She slipped farther beneath the water and blew bubbles.

Or it could be that for some reason, in some weird way he reminded her of her baby's father.

Nina zipped up her jacket to her chin and made the last turn into town. The brisk walk from the B and B into the town center had done her good. The fifteen-minute walk had cleared her head and relaxed her more than the warm bath had.

She hadn't completely shrugged off her big-city addiction, and the thought of spending a quiet evening at home just sounded like a big bore.

The locals usually liked to gather at Mandy's Café for dinner or at one of two watering holes that hadn't become tourist traps—yet. The island had changed a lot since the last time she'd really spent time here. At least the crowds had allowed Mom and Dad to run a flourishing business, but Break Island didn't offer the complete serenity she'd hoped for.

Maybe that was a good thing. The warmth and conversation that enfolded her as soon as she stepped across the threshold of Mandy's felt like a friendly hug. And she could use a few of those.

She tripped to a stop when she saw Jase Buckley at the center of a lively group in the corner. Hadn't he just arrived in town? She kept tabs on him out of the corner of her eye as she slid into a booth by the window. He must be a good writer, because he sure seemed to have the gift of the gab over there, spinning stories for an enthralled audience.

"Do you want something to drink, Nina?" Theresa Kennedy, one of her mother's old friends, tapped a pencil against her pad of paper. Theresa's family had owned Mandy's for years.

"Just water, but I'll take a cup of the chicken noodle soup right now."

"You got it. So, are you really going to fix up the old place? We could use another B and B on the island."

"I am, but I'm going to take my time, so I hope you're not in any hurry."

"It'll go faster with my help."

Theresa stepped back to allow Jase to sidle up to the table. "Are you going to help Nina get the place back on its feet?"

"Starting tomorrow."

Theresa poked Jase in the chest with the eraser end of her pencil. "I hope that doesn't cut into your writing time, Jase."

Nina raised her eyebrows. Had the guy spilled his life story all over town? Perhaps the connection she'd felt with him had been nothing more than Jase being Jase. "I'll have plenty of time, Theresa." He winked. "A man's gotta eat, too."

"Oh, go on. You could come in here and I'd feed you

anytime of the day or night. It would just be like having my son home again when he was studying for the bar. Anyway, I think it's a good idea for you to lend a hand to Nina."

"Nina needs help and I need work, so it's a perfect fit."

"Nina does need help." Theresa cocked her head to one side like one of the birds from the island's sanctuary. "But for the life of me, I still can't figure out why she abandoned her exciting life in LA for this old place."

"Sometimes we all just need a break. Maybe Nina needs a break."

"Hello." Nina waved her hands between Jase and Theresa. "I'm right here. No need to talk about me like I'm not."

Theresa clucked her tongue. "I'll get you that soup, Nina. Jase?"

"I'll take some soup, too." He patted the back of the banquette across from her. "Do you mind if I join you?"

Her gaze flicked to the table of locals still bunched together. "Is your audience going to miss you?"

"Them?" He snorted. "They're on to the next tall tale."

"And you?"

"Tall tales? I've told my share." He slipped into the booth across from her. "Did you finally warm up?"

"I did a little work around the house and then took a warm bath. That did the trick."

"Any more news about your sister?"

"Stepsister. I was going to ask around town tonight if anyone has seen her today." She rubbed her hands together when she spotted Theresa backing out of the kitchen with a cup of soup in each hand. "But not before I had some sustenance."

Theresa placed the soup in front of them, along with a basket of crackers. "Do you want to order now?"

Nina didn't have to look at the menu. "I'll have the fish-and-chips."

"I'll have the same." Jase tapped the edge of the plastic menu on the table. "And another beer, Theresa, that pale ale."

"You got it. Just water for you, Nina?"

"That's it."

When Theresa took their menus and walked away, Jase asked, "You don't mind if I have a beer, do you?"

"Why should I?" She blinked and then planted her elbows on the table. "You don't think I'm an alcoholic, do you?"

"No."

"Because I leave all the drinking in the family to my stepsister."

Jase raised a spoonful of hot soup to his lips and blew on the puddle. "Just didn't want to make you uncomfortable in case you're a rabid teetotaler."

She was no rabid teetotaler, whatever that meant, but the way Jase's lips puckered made her plenty uncomfortable. She shifted in her seat and busied herself with the wrapper on a package of crackers.

"Drink all you want. Be my guest."

"I'd like to be your guest."

Her soup went down the wrong way and she coughed. Pressing a napkin to her lips, she asked, "What?"

"You run a B and B, don't you?"

"We've established that." She sniffed and dabbed her eyes. "But you've seen the condition it's in. It's hardly ready for prime time."

"It would work out great for me—and you. I could stay in one of the rooms, do work around the place every day and get my writing done in a much better setting than my current location at The Sandpiper." He crumbled a cracker into his bowl and then dusted his hands off over a napkin. "You could pay me in room and board instead of cash. It's a win-win for both of us."

"Although I already hired you, I still want to do a background check on you." After months of being on edge, how had she allowed Jase to lure her into feelings of security already? She still needed to remain vigilant. Simon could be anywhere.

"Check away." He thanked Theresa for the beer and took a swig from the bottle. "My life's an open book."

She wished she could say the same. Keeping her pregnancy a secret from Jase and everyone else in town was silly. They'd find out soon enough. She ran a finger along the inside of her tight waistband. Like in about two days when she made the switch to maternity clothes. She'd already done a little shopping in Seattle on her way to the island.

Theresa delivered their platters of fish-and-chips and conversation came to a dead halt as they busied themselves with lemons, vinegar and tartar sauce.

Nina bit into the crispy coating of the fish and closed her eyes as the salty, tart tastes flooded her mouth.

"I think this meal alone is worth coming all the way out here for." Jase swept a French fry through a mountain of ketchup on his plate. "Is this why you returned to the old homestead?"

"Mandy's fish-and-chips?" She laughed. "Yeah, that's it."

They finished their meal and split the check. How had Jase known that's exactly how she'd wanted to handle it? If he'd insisted on paying, it would've felt too much like a date—and it already felt too much like a date.

When they hit the sidewalk, she thrust out her hand. "You're coming by tomorrow to go over the necessary repairs, right?"

"Sure." He took her hand but didn't release it. "I'll walk you to your car."

"Car?" She raised her eyebrows. "I'm not in LA anymore. I walked over here."

His grip tightened on her hand. "Really? I'll walk you home, then."

As her eyes traveled over his shoulder to take in the dark curve of the sand dunes that marked the turn toward the B and B, she said, "That's not necessary," but her voice didn't hold the conviction she'd wanted.

Would Simon track her down here? If he wanted to speak with her, he should just approach her like a normal person. But Simon hadn't been normal the past few times she'd seen him—not normal at all.

He shrugged. "I don't mind the walk."

"It *is* a nice walk."

They turned together and after two blocks the sidewalk ended in sand. He put his hand on the small of her back. "Be careful."

She appreciated Jase's solicitousness, but she didn't understand it. Why was he so attentive? It was almost as if he knew about her pregnancy.

She stole a sideways glance at his perfectly chiseled profile. *Idiot.* Maybe he did know she was pregnant. Just because she hadn't made the switch to maternity clothes yet, it didn't mean people couldn't tell. That woman in the elevator at the doctor's office knew. She was pretty sure Carl and Dora Kleinschmidt knew.

She cleared her throat. "You never did tell me why you chose Break Island for your writer's retreat."

"Do I have to explain?" He spread his arms. "It's isolated, beautiful, but has just enough tourists for some serious people-watching for inspiration."

"I thought you were writing a fictional account of your

experiences in Afghanistan—not many soldiers here to study." Unless Simon was lurking around the corner.

"They don't have to be soldiers. Human nature is human nature."

A bush rustled beside them and a gust of wind showered them with grains of sand.

Then a figure stepped onto the path in front of them and a voice came out of the night. "Home at last."

Chapter Five

Nina stiffened beside him, and Jase's own muscles coiled as he sprang in front of her, blocking her from the stranger on the path.

A low laugh gurgled from the woman's throat. "That's our Nina, always has a man to protect her."

Nina placed a hand on his arm and stepped beside him. "Are you stalking me, Lou?"

Instead of diffusing his concern, the fact that it was Nina's stepsister standing in front of them blocking their path heightened it. Lou had put a hole in Nina's boat, and even if Nina had been convinced the act wouldn't have resulted in her drowning, he didn't trust this woman anywhere near Nina.

"Stalking?" She took in the bay with a sweeping gesture. "I'm just enjoying the night like everyone else."

"Have you been working on Dad's boat by any chance?" Nina squared her shoulders and locked eyes with her stepsister, whom she topped by a good five inches. In hand-to-hand battle, he'd put his money on Nina any day—except she was pregnant.

"Moi?" Lou crossed her hands over her heart. "I haven't touched *my* dad's boat, and don't go calling him *Dad* like he's your dad or something. Your dad took off

a few months after you were born, having the good sense to dump you and Lori while he could."

"Hey." Jase curled his hands into fists and took a step forward. "Don't talk to Nina like that. I don't care who you are."

"And I don't care who *you* are." Lou put a hand on her hip, her gaze raking him from head to toe. "Who *are* you?"

"This is my…my handyman, Jase. He's going to help me fix up Moonstones."

What had Nina been about to call him? Handyman sounded so impersonal.

Lou leveled a finger at Nina. "That B and B should be mine and you know it. That's why you left it so long after my dad died. You felt guilty about inheriting it."

"We both know what would've happened to Moonstones if Dad had left it to you. Dad knew it, too. You would've sold this place so fast and used the money for God-knows-what. I can get it up and running again, and I have no problem sharing the profits with you if there are any."

"None of that matters. I don't want the piddly profits from some mom-and-pop business." Lou sliced her hand through the air a little too close to Nina's face for his comfort. "I could've used the money. You didn't need it with your stuck-up interior designing job in LA. Why did you give up all that to come back here anyway?"

Jase studied Nina's face as she formed an answer. So, her stepsister didn't know about the pregnancy, either, but he didn't blame Nina for not telling her. Lou had nut job written all over her.

In the end, Nina shrugged. "Moonstones needs some TLC. Dad and Mom loved the place."

"My dad had this dream before he met Lori, before he left my mom for her."

Nina sighed and ran her hands through her hair. "We've been over and over this, Lou. I'm sorry that happened, but it has nothing to do with us."

"It does now because Dad disinherited me for you. I always hoped Lori would die before Dad because I thought Dad would cut you out. Lori did die first, but Dad cut me out anyway." Her laugh sounded just this side of hysterical. "So, you gypped me out of my inheritance *and* my father."

"I'm sorry about that, too, Lou. They were the loves of each other's lives. You and I both know they loved each other more than they loved their daughters." Nina crossed her arms over her stomach. "Sometimes life just works out that way."

"Oh, you can be generous because you got the goods after Dad kicked off."

"Lou, baby? Lou, you out here?"

The slurred words came out of the darkness, along with a shuffling gait.

What now? As if all this family drama wasn't enough. "Over here, Kip."

A lean man with tousled sandy hair came up from the beach, listing to the side as he scrambled up to the path. The stink of stale beer came off him in waves.

He staggered to Lou's side and draped a heavy arm across her shoulders.

"This is my stepsister, Nina, the golden child. Nina, this is Kip, my partner in crime."

Keeping her feet rooted to the ground, Nina leaned in with an outstretched hand. "Good to meet you, Kip, but Lou doesn't need a partner in crime."

Ignoring the proffered handshake, Kip hacked and spit into the sand dunes. "Just a figure of speech."

Nina nodded in Jase's direction. "And this is Jase."

Jase held up one hand. He had no intention of shaking

with Kip. The guy might topple over on him in a drunken free fall.

Nina continued to pretend this was some normal social gathering.

"Where did you and Lou meet?"

"In a bar." Kip pulled Lou in for a sloppy kiss on the side of the head.

"I meant—" Nina rolled her eyes "—what city?"

"Portland." Lou brushed a sandy lock of hair from Kip's eyes. "I've been living in Portland."

"Are you staying here now?"

"Just in town at one of the dumpy fishermen's motels." She clicked her tongue. "Don't worry, little sis. It's not going to be permanent. I have some business to settle."

Jase studied Lou and Kip side by side through narrowed eyes. The only business he could imagine these two settling is a drug deal. That, or harassing Nina.

He took Nina's arm. "We were just on our way back to Moonstones."

"And we were on our way back to the bar." Kip tugged on Lou's hand. "Come on, baby. Let's finish gettin' our drink on."

The other couple squeezed past them on the path to make their way back to the town. Once again, Jase caught a strong whiff of booze. Had Kip bathed in it?

When Kip and Lou disappeared into the night, Nina let out a long breath. "I can't believe she'd hook up with someone like that."

"Seems to me old Kip is just her type."

She pulled her jacket around her body. "Lou needs help, professional help. I don't understand people who refuse to seek therapy and medication when it's glaringly obvious to everyone around them that they need them."

"I'm not sure. I've heard the drugs flatten out your personality, and people don't like that."

"Some personalities need flattening."

"Lou sure holds a grudge, doesn't she?" A bird, probably an escapee from the sanctuary, shrieked above them and Nina jumped.

"Where's her mother?"

"Lou's mom has been through a couple of husbands already. She could be anywhere, since she pretty much washed her hands of Lou, too." She kicked at a rock with the toe of her shoe. "One thing Lou did have right is that her father left her mother for my mom."

"That's not your fault."

"Lou instinctively knew the score when she was nine years old. She hated me and my mom from the get-go."

"Nine is old enough. Did your stepfather prefer you to his own daughter?"

"Not really—he preferred my mom and my mom preferred him. I was a lot easier to deal with than Lou, and Dad knew she'd sell Moonstones as soon as she could and then drink up, snort up and shoot up the profits."

The road curved in front of the disputed B and B, and a glimmer of light from the quarter moon spilled across Nina's disabled boat.

"Lou denied sabotaging the boat."

Nina snorted. "Did you think she'd admit it? She's never fessed up to a single misdeed in her life."

"You have a complicated life, Nina." He opened the latch of the broken gate and ushered her through with a sweep of his hand.

"You have no idea, Jase."

He held his breath as she moved past him, her light fragrance tickling his nose. Would she tell him about her pregnancy? Open up about Simon?

She climbed the two porch steps and turned to face him.

He held her gaze, ready for her confidences. Not that

he'd be sharing any of his own—revealing his identity was not part of his assignment—yet.

"You know that proposal you made over dinner?"

He blinked. Not what he'd been expecting, but he'd go with it. "About moving in here?"

"Yes. Still interested?"

"Sure."

"Good." She turned and shoved open the front door of the B and B. "Because I want you to move in—right here, right now."

THE THRILL THAT rushed through his body better be for the assignment and not the woman. She'd done a one-eighty and ditched her previous reservations. Had Lou spooked her?

"Why the sudden turnaround?"

"Do you see it that way? I told you I'd consider it after doing a background check."

"And now you don't need a background check?"

"Now I've seen Lou and the company she's keeping."

"Do you really think Kip is helping her? The dude seems barely capable of a coherent thought."

"I've seen his type before. Lou's been with this type before—they egg her on and use her because they think she has some money coming. They encourage her in her wild schemes."

"He scares you?"

"They both do. Did you see his eyebrows?"

He raised one of his own. "I didn't notice."

"They were lighter than his hair."

"Is that supposed to be some sign of evil or some-thing?"

She pinched his arm. "He gave me the creeps."

"Okay, I defer to your creep meter, but if you want me

to move in tonight, I'm going to have to go back to my motel and get my stuff."

"I'll take you back in my truck. You can start some repairs tomorrow and write whenever you want."

"And run interference between you and Lou and Kip. Is that it?"

"If you don't mind."

"I don't mind at all." He came here for that express purpose—to run interference for Nina Moore—not that she knew it.

"Hold on and I'll get the keys to the truck." She left him standing at the door while she ran to the kitchen and snagged a set of keys from a hook.

The driver's-side door of the truck protested when he opened it for her. "Is there anything at Moonstones that's *not* falling apart?"

"No, and that includes the current owner." She hopped onto the seat and slammed the door.

He climbed in beside her. "If it's too much for you, Nina, why don't you go back to LA? Lou seemed to think you had it made there."

"Lou?" She adjusted her mirror. "You believe anything Lou says?"

"Does that mean you *didn't* have it made in LA?"

She bit her lip before starting and once again he expected confidences.

"I liked my job, had plenty of clients and left a lot of friends there, but this island has something…"

"A dilapidated B and B and crazy family members."

He didn't know why he was trying to encourage her to return to the big city. It would be so much harder to watch her there, and what possible excuse could he offer now for turning up in LA?

She laughed and he liked the sound. She needed to laugh more—for the baby.

"With your help, Moonstones won't be dilapidated for long and hopefully Lou will be on her way, taking her low-life companion with her."

"Once she finishes her important business."

She swung the truck onto the road leading to town, a smirk twisting her lips. "I'm afraid her important business is getting me to cough up some money."

"Will you? Have you ever?"

"I've given her a few bucks here and there, but that only seems to encourage her. Honestly, I do it out of guilt."

"Because your mom stole her dad away from her mom? That's ridiculous."

"I know it is. I just know how it feels to lose a parent." She glanced at him. "You heard Lou. My dad abandoned me and my mom when I was a baby."

"For another woman?"

"I have no clue, but my mom raised me alone until Bruce Moore came into her life." Her hands tightened on the steering wheel. "A baby needs two parents, don't you think?"

He licked his dry lips. "It's optimal."

As if sensing something in his tone, she turned to him. "Have you ever been married? I'm assuming you're not now because, well, you don't wear a ring and I can't imagine your wife being okay with you escaping for a few months to write."

"I am not now, nor have I ever been married."

"Children?"

"None that I know of." He didn't feel like talking about babies right now—hers or his.

Nina nodded once. Then she wheeled into the space in front of his motel room and threw the old truck into Park. "Do you need any help packing up?"

"It'll take me five minutes." He jumped from the truck

and five minutes later with his laptop tucked under his arm, he tossed his duffel into the back of the truck.

When he climbed into the passenger seat, Nina was texting on her cell.

"Everything okay?"

She held up the phone. "Still putting the finishing touches on a client's house in Malibu—job from hell."

"You should be able to do right by Moonstones with your expertise."

"Yeah, but I need a clean palette to work with, not a place falling down around my ears."

"That's where I come in."

It took her three tries before the engine cranked to life, and she looked over her shoulder before backing out of the space.

"How'd a soldier and a writer wind up being handy with a hammer and saw?"

"I learned everything from my grandfather. He liked working with his hands, even after..." He tugged on his ear before the truth came spilling from his lips. "Even after he got old."

He didn't need to clue in Nina that his grandfather had been a self-made millionaire and that his father had expanded the family fortunes and gone into politics. That reality wouldn't mesh with Jase Buckley's.

"Do you mind if we make a stop before heading back to the B and B? I need to pick up a couple of things."

"There's a drugstore on the main drag, a few doors down from Mandy's." She swung the truck around in a U-turn and rumbled back down the main street of town.

When she parked, he grabbed the handle of the door. "You coming with me?"

"Sure."

As they walked inside the brightly lit drugstore, the

clerk behind the register called out, "You have ten minutes until closing."

"We'll make it quick." Jase nudged Nina with his elbow. "Toothpaste."

They rounded the corner of the aisle, which gave them a straight shot to the pharmacy counter, where a couple was arguing with the pharmacist.

"I think someone else was using my driver's license."

"I don't think so, ma'am."

"God, don't call me ma'am. I'm only thirty-one."

Nina tugged on his sleeve to try to escape her stepsister's notice, but Lou caught the movement and turned.

"Nina, can you help me out?"

"Ma'am… Miss, you can't have someone buy the antihistamine for you after just trying to buy it yourself."

Lou cussed at the pharmacist and slapped the counter. "Hick town."

"C'mon, babe. Let's go back to the bar." Kip, looking more beat-up than before, wrapped an arm around Lou's waist.

"Hold on." She shrugged him off. "What are you doing back in town, Nina? I thought you were headed to Moonstones."

"Needed a few things." Nina tipped her chin toward the pharmacist, who was hastily rolling down his window.

"Why are you trying to buy antihistamines?"

"You know, runny nose." Lou pinched the bridge of her nose and sniffed.

"Antihistamines are for stuffed-up noses."

Lou plucked a tube of lip balm from a hook and put it in her pocket. "You have any room at the inn?"

"What?" Nina visibly recoiled.

"At Moonstones? Any vacancies for me and Kip to crash?"

"I…I thought you were staying here in town."

"We are, but we're running out of cash."

Jase reached his arm behind Nina and gave her hip a pinch. Surely, she could say no to her stepsister. The woman tried to drown her just this afternoon.

"I can't help you, Lou."

"Of course not. You got what was rightfully mine, and now you can't even spare a room for me."

"Jase and I were expecting to be alone."

His heart slammed against his chest. What was she playing at?

Lou narrowed her reddened eyes. "You and your handyman?"

Nina tossed back her shoulder-length hair. "I just didn't want to get you all wound up, Lou, but I'm getting sick of tiptoeing around you."

"What does that mean?" Lou's voice had taken on a dangerous edge, and Jase inched closer to Nina.

"Jase isn't my handyman. He's my fiancé."

Chapter Six

Nina wrapped her arm around Jase and gave him a squeeze. It was what she'd been wanting to do ever since he pulled her from the water anyway. Now she had an excuse.

Kip had dropped the box of condoms he'd been fidgeting with, and Lou gave it a kick with the toe of her shoe.

Nina's muscles went rigid, bracing for the explosion.

Lou's trembling lips stretched into a line and then turned up at one corner. "I'm not as surprised as you might think."

Not as surprised as Jase anyway, who hadn't uttered a sound since her announcement of their impending nuptials.

"And why is that, Lou?"

"I'd heard you were engaged, but that was through a friend of an acquaintance's second cousin or something like that, so I didn't know how true it was."

Lou had heard about Simon? Nina squared her shoulders. "Well, it's true, and we want to be alone, so you'll have to tough it out at your motel."

"I wouldn't expect anything more of you, sis."

A low sound rumbled in Jase's throat and he pulled her close. "Now that I'm going to be part of the family,

I can speak my mind. You need to stop ragging on Nina and get your life together."

"Really." Lou crossed her arms and her light-colored eyes glittered.

Even though Lou self-medicated with drugs and booze, those substances did nothing to calm her down. But Nina had Jase to protect her until Lou left the island. She hoped he understood the lie. He seemed to be taking to it like a natural.

"And we don't want to see any more damaged boats or anything like it."

Lou spun around and grabbed Kip by the arm. "Whatever. You two deserve each other, but just beware, Jase. Nina will use you and then chew you up and spit you out."

"Folks." The clerk was standing at the end of the aisle, her eyes wide. "We're closed."

Jase waved his toothpaste in the air. "I still need to buy my toothpaste."

"Hurry it up, and you two—" she wagged a finger between Lou and Kip "—you need to leave."

They left without a backward glance, Kip leaning heavily on Lou.

Aware of the cashier glancing from her face to Jase's, Nina kept her mouth shut as Jase paid for his toothpaste and they walked out of the store.

Not until they climbed into the truck and Nina cranked on the engine did Jase whistle through his teeth.

"Sorry, sorry." She put her hand on his thigh. "It wasn't just a way to get her to stop trying to wiggle into Moonstones—it was a message to her that I wasn't alone. I hope you don't mind too much. If she follows her usual pattern, she'll throw a few temper tantrums and then leave the island when she doesn't get her way, and hopefully take that creepy Kip with her."

"I'm okay with it just as long as you don't start shopping for rings."

The hand on his thigh curled into a fist and she punched him. "Don't worry."

After they returned to the B and B and she'd shown him to the one decent room and bathroom, she lay on top of her covers in a pair of flannel pj's, rubbing her belly.

The stress of seeing Lou today couldn't be good for the baby.

Had her stepsister been watching and waiting for her to return to Break Island? Did she have spies here reporting to her?

She rolled to her left side and buried her face in the pillow. Now she sounded as paranoid as Lou.

At least seeing her stepsister today convinced her that the hole in the boat was not the work of Simon. And why would it be? What did Simon have to gain from giving her a scare?

She'd escaped from LA to Break Island for relaxation and simplicity, but her problems had not only followed her, they'd multiplied.

Now she didn't have to face them alone. She had Jase Buckley on her side.

She tucked her hand beneath her cheek. She didn't even know the man. Why did he make her feel so safe? The boat rescue was only part of it. He reminded her of Simon—before the PTSD had taken control of Simon's mind—steady, strong, loyal, lethal.

Lethal? Where had that come from?

Simon had always insisted he held a boring government job developing security systems, but she'd never believed him because he traveled a lot and never discussed his work or coworkers—except that one she met, Max Duvall, who'd been as mysterious as Simon. Maybe she'd let her imagination carry her away, but she'd had a hard time believing Simon was a pencil-pushing civil servant.

Maybe if he had been, the PTSD wouldn't have destroyed him.

And Jase? Was he more than he appeared to be?

Right now he was her pretend-fiancé—and that was good enough. But shouldn't even a pretend-fiancé know that his pretend-fiancée was pregnant?

SHE WOKE UP the next morning to the sound of a saw. She shoved her feet into a pair of fuzzy slippers and scuffed across the floor to the front rooms. She peeked through the curtains at Jase sawing wood, the old fence torn down and lying in a heap.

He had shed his flannel, and his muscles bunched and flexed beneath his white T-shirt as he worked. As if sensing her scrutiny, he looked up from the fence.

No good pretending she hadn't been staring. She raised her hand and he waved back.

Tucking her robe around her body, she opened the front door and stepped onto the porch. "How long have you been at it?"

"About an hour. Did I wake you?"

"No. You've made a lot of progress. Do you want some breakfast?"

"Isn't this a bed-and-breakfast?"

"Yeah."

"Then I'd like some breakfast."

She put a hand on her hip. "It's not like you're a regular guest."

"That's right. I'm your fiancé." He picked up his saw and started attacking the next piece of wood.

She let the door slam behind her as she stepped back into the house. Brushing her hands together, she made a beeline for the kitchen. Her mom had been a great cook, but she hadn't inherited that cooking gene. If she ever got this place back on its feet, she planned to hire a chef to cook the meals for the guests.

But she had a guest now, and he had to be hungry after working for an hour on the fence.

She rustled up enough ingredients for an omelet and made some toast to go with it. She put the kettle on for tea but Jase had mentioned relying on a cup of coffee to get him going in the morning. She hadn't drunk much coffee even when she wasn't pregnant and she didn't want to pump the baby full of caffeine, so she didn't even have any instant coffee to offer him.

She poked her head out the front door. "I don't have any coffee. I can run into town and get you a cup at Logan's Coffee."

He reached for the top of a post and held up a white cup with a sleeve wrapped around it. "Beat you to it. I told you I needed a shot of caffeine in the morning to give me a jump start. Do you think I could've accomplished all this without it?"

"Impressive. Are you ready for breakfast?"

"You don't have to call me twice." Holding his cup in one hand, he stepped over a pile of debris and met her on the porch.

"Let me wash my hands and I'll be right with you."

She set the table as the water ran in the bathroom and then Jase emerged, buttoning up a different flannel from the one he wore yesterday.

She circled a finger in front of him. "Do you think a flannel shirt is the state shirt of Washington or something?"

He laughed and tugged on the collar. "If it is, it's for a good reason. It's chilly up here, and I have a feeling it's going to get worse with that storm on the way."

"It's supposed to be a monster." She sat down and broke

off a corner of toast. She'd passed the stage in her pregnancy for queasiness, but hadn't yet broken the habit of nibbling on dry toast.

"Where are you from, Jase? I detect a little bit of a New England accent."

"Really?" He selected a piece of toast from the plate as if he was picking out a new car. Then he spread a pat of butter across the surface in slow motion.

"Yeah, really. Are you from the Northeast?"

He shrugged. "Connecticut."

"And what did you do in Connecticut before your stint as a marine?

"I taught high school history for a year before enlisting and went back to that when I got out before I decided I needed to write down my experiences."

"Were they bad?"

"What? Who?" He crunched into the toast.

"Your experiences." She swirled the tea bag in the hot water, watching the ripples spread across the surface. "Did you have bad experiences during the war?"

"It was war, but it wasn't all bad and my book is mostly about that part—the not-bad part." He took a pull from his coffee cup. "How about your... stepfather? Did he talk about it much?"

"He was in Vietnam. I think it affected him deeply. He suffered from depression."

"Is that why he…?"

"Killed himself?" She took a quick slurp of tea, burning her tongue in the process. "I'm sure that contributed to it. My mom was his lifeline, so when he lost her he felt as if he'd lost everything, even his will to live."

He shook his head. "That's either a great love, or that's obsession."

"They are different, aren't they?"

"Definitely." He picked a mushroom out of his omelet

and pushed it to the side of his plate. "Have you ever had either one?"

A smile curved her lip as she resisted laying a hand on her tummy. "Yeah. How about you?"

His brown eyes darkened to black as he stared past her. "I thought I did."

"I've been there, too." She sighed and picked up her fork, aiming it at his plate. "You don't like mushrooms?"

"No."

"Sorry. I should've asked."

He brushed off her apology with a wave of his fork. "No problem. This is a good omelet with all the other stuff in it."

"What's up after the fence?"

"Thought I'd start clearing some of the weeds in the front and maybe do some repairs on that deck."

"I've got a guy lined up for the gardening, but I'd love to have that deck back online. My parents loved sitting out there in front of a fire and watching the bay."

"I can see why. It's a great spot." He shook his empty coffee cup. "Do you think our ruse was enough to get you off Lou's radar for now?"

"Maybe. Again, I apologize for the drastic measures. I just wanted to let her know that I wasn't alone, that I had someone...on my side."

"I am on your side, Nina."

"Why, Jase?" She planted her elbows on the table and rested her chin on her folded hands. "Why have you been so helpful to a total stranger?"

He cocked his head. "I think it's just the circumstances. I was there when your boat sprang a leak, and I was there again when you ran into your evil stepsister and her creepy companion. I'm not here completely out of the goodness of my heart. This is the perfect place for me to set up shop for a little while."

"Are you saying if I didn't have this B and B, you'd have let me sink in the bay?"

"I wouldn't have let anyone sink in that bay—including Lou and Kip."

"I'm just teasing. You have some natural protective instincts, just like…"

"Your stepfather?"

Her stepfather's only protective instincts had been toward his wife, but Simon had wanted to save everyone. Until he couldn't save himself.

"Yeah, my stepfather was pretty protective."

"Maybe it's a military thing."

"Yeah, a military thing."

"Are you going to be working around the B and B, or do you have other plans for the day?"

"I'd like to head across the bay today like I was trying to do yesterday, to get some supplies."

"Are you going to take the ferry?"

"I am."

"Are you going to be able to haul back everything that you need?"

"Not as much as I could with a boat, but I'll manage. The mainland provides carts for the islanders, especially now with the storm on its way."

"Do you want me to come along?"

"When do you write?"

A muscle in his jaw twitched. "I'll do some writing tonight."

"I can go it alone." She pushed back from the table and grabbed their empty plates. "You have your work cut out for you here."

"Do you need a ride to the ferry dock?"

"I was just going to drive and park, unless you think you need the truck for something."

"I might need it, if that's okay."

"Sure, I'm sorry I didn't think of it."

"That's not why I offered to drive you." He plucked the keys from the hook on the cabinet. "Never mind. It's a good enough reason."

There it was again. He'd been looking out for her. She might as well accept it and go with the flow.

When Jase pulled up in front of the dock, he reached into his pocket and pulled out a slip of paper. "You could use a few things for the yard unless your gardener had it covered, that is, if you have room in your cart."

She took the slip of paper from his fingers and dropped it into her purse. "I'm sure Brian's going to need supplies and tools for the yard. He's not really a gardener, just a dropout from U-dub, and there will be plenty of room on the cart. People do this all the time. Not everyone has a boat, believe it or not."

"I'd hate to be stuck on an island and dependent on the ferry to get off and on."

"Lots of people do it, but Mom and Dad always had a boat." She popped the door handle before Jase had a chance to hop out and get her door. He'd really go overboard if he knew she was pregnant.

Not that she minded his attentions, but if she planned to embark on single motherhood, she'd better get used to managing on her own.

He sat in the idling truck until she boarded the ferry and turned to wave. As the ferry chugged across the bay, she kept her eyes on the truck until it turned into a toy.

He'd watched her across the water, and she'd watched him. What was this connection they had? She didn't know whether to feel relieved or nervous that it didn't seem to be all one-sided.

The ferry cut through the bay, heading toward Newport. It was the closest thing Break Island had to a big city. It did have a big-box store, and that's all she needed for now.

As she walked down the gangplank, her tennis shoes squeaking on the metal, she nodded to a couple of Break Island locals waiting in line for the ferry back.

She snagged a taxi and bypassed Newport's tourist shops on the way to the working area of the city.

The driver eyed her in the rearview mirror. "On a supply run from one of the islands to get ready for the storm?"

"Break."

"That's a pretty one. My mother likes that bird sanctuary."

"Are you a local?"

"Naw. Came out here from Portland to get away from it all. You know?"

"I do know." As the big-box store came into view, she pulled some cash from her purse. "Your mom's here, too?"

"She just visits once in a while, but Break Island's her favorite because of that sanctuary."

She wished the entire island was a sanctuary. "You can just drop me in front."

"I'd offer to wait, but you're probably going to need one of the vans to get all your stuff back to the ferry."

"Yeah, I'll call in when I'm done shopping." She paid the driver and whipped out her membership card for the store as she marched up to the entrance. She grabbed a cart and maneuvered up and down the aisles, with a mind toward feeding a guest.

If Jase planned on doing physical labor all day and mental labor all night, he needed more than a vegetarian omelet for breakfast.

She'd gotten over her morning sickness and queasiness pretty quickly and could stomach just about anything now—except peanut butter. One sandwich early on in her pregnancy that hadn't gone down well had turned her off peanut butter for good.

She parked her cart in the meat aisle and hunched over the refrigerated display, evaluating the different cuts of meat. Jase looked like someone who might be picky just because of that patrician air he wore around him. His actual actions couldn't be further from a high-maintenance guy's, but he just seemed so darned perfect.

A flash of red hair caught her attention, and she jerked her head around. Two little dark-haired kids jostled for position in front of a free-sample table—no redheads in sight.

She patted her belly. Would this little one have red hair? She couldn't imagine anything cuter.

She continued to load her cart and changed lines twice to find the shortest one. Resigning herself to the wait, she hung on her cart and watched the stream of people in and out of the store.

Her heart jumped when her eyes locked on to a tall, broad man with red hair leaving the store.

She climbed on the edge of the cart and craned her neck for a better look. She shouted, "Simon."

A few people threw curious glances her way, and her cheeks warmed under their scrutiny. Calling out to him didn't make any sense, since her voice couldn't carry that far, especially with the noise level in the big warehouse.

If that were Simon, would he even turn around if he heard her? In all the weeks she'd suspected him of stalking her in LA, he'd never once attempted to make contact with her.

That's what frightened her. Why play games? Their breakup hadn't been that acrimonious, not at the end anyway. What led up to it, however...

She shivered and hugged herself.

"Miss?"

She glanced over her shoulder at the anxious face of a grandmotherly type. "Yes?"

"You can move ahead now."

She rolled her cart into the gap between her and the next cart with her heart thumping in her chest. First Lou and now Simon. Who *wouldn't* show up here in Washington?

She shook her head. There were tall men in the world with red hair, even here in Washington.

She transferred several items from her cart to the conveyor belt and left the big stuff in the basket. Once she'd checked out, she rushed to the exit and scanned the crowds of people eating in the outdoor food court area. No redheads.

She blew out a breath and shoved her cart in front of her. She'd been like this in LA, too—seeing red-haired men all over the place.

She ordered a taxi van to the dock and waited for it at the edge of the parking lot. When the yellow van arrived, the driver helped her load her supplies in the back.

"Which island are you from?"

"Break."

"Haven't been out to that one so much."

"It's quiet."

"Aren't they all?"

"Some more than others."

He hit the main drag, lined with T-shirt and trinket shops, and traffic slowed to a crawl. "Everyone over from the islands trying to stock up before the big storm hits."

"Uh-huh." Nina pressed her nose against the window, her gaze tracking back and forth along the sidewalks.

"Looking for someone?"

She peeled herself off the glass and slumped back in her seat. "No."

The driver rolled up behind a line of taxis in front of the harbor. "You need a pallet cart for this stuff?"

"Yeah, I do." She slid open the door. "Wait here and I'll grab one."

She weaved through knots of people on the wharf to claim a cart. As she dug into her pocket for the five-dollar bill that would rent the cart, someone grabbed her arm.

She spun around, her jaw clenched and her hands balled up into fists.

"Whoa!" Jase held out his hands. "I wasn't going to steal your cart."

"Jase." She swallowed. "You scared me."

"Obviously." He studied her face with his eyebrows meeting over his nose.

"What are you doing here?"

"I borrowed the Kleinschmidts' boat."

"Again? They're going to have you arrested."

"I asked them this time, and they said we could use it until yours is repaired. I figured I'd save you the hassle of lugging this stuff on a cart onto the ferry and then loading up the truck on the other side. The boat will take you practically to your doorstep."

"Great, thanks." She stuffed a still-trembling hand into her pocket. "The stuff's in the taxi."

"We'll get the cart anyway to transport it from the taxi to the boat, since I can't get the boat any closer to the ferry terminal."

She let him deal with the cart and led the way to the waiting taxi.

Jase and the driver loaded up the supplies, and after paying the driver, she helped Jase steer the cart toward the slip where he'd docked the Kleinschmidts' boat.

As she lifted a bag of fertilizer, Jase stopped her. "I'll get that."

"What *won't* you get?" He'd grabbed every item heavier than a feather out of her arms.

"Nothing." He flicked his fingers at her. "Go get the boat ready for departure and make sure this stuff is secure enough on the deck."

She saluted. "Aye, aye, Captain."

While she was mumbling about bossy men, she lifted her head to brush the hair from her face and saw the weak sun glinting off a redhead in line for the ferry.

A surge of anger thumped through her veins, and she jumped from the boat.

"Nina?" Jase called after her, but her single-mindedness drove her feet in the direction of the ferry.

Reaching the end of the line for the boat, she began pushing her way through, ignoring the comments and protests.

"Hey! Hey, you! Simon!"

As she reached the redhead and grabbed handfuls of his jacket, he jerked around.

Nina met a pair of cornflower blue eyes and stumbled back.

The man grabbed her arm. "You must be Nina Moore."

Chapter Seven

Jase reached Nina just in time to pull her away from the redheaded stranger's grasp. She collapsed against him, her face pale and her lips trembling.

The man's eyes darted to Jase's face, and he spread his hands in front of him. "Just catching her fall."

"Who is this, Nina?" Jase wrapped his arm around Nina's waist, curling it around her front.

"I…I don't know. I thought he was…someone else, but he knows my name."

The man's face turned almost the same shade as his hair as he jerked his thumb over his shoulder. "Can we talk about this somewhere else?"

"Spill it now. You're going to miss your ferry." Jase nodded toward the front of the line shuffling toward the gangplank.

"Doesn't matter. This ferry is going to Break Island. I was on my way to see Nina anyway."

Nina's body froze and she clawed at Jase's wrist. "Why? Who are you? What do you want?"

"He's right, Nina. Let's continue this conversation out of this line. We're going to start holding people up."

They jostled their way out of the line, and Jase pointed toward the Kleinschmidts' boat. "We have a boat over here."

The stranger followed them, as Nina shrank against Jase's side. Why was she so afraid of him? Just because he knew her name?

When they got to the boat, Jase balanced one foot on the pallet while still holding onto Nina. "So, who are you and what do you want with Nina?"

"Nina." The man turned to face her. "I'm Simon Skinner's brother."

Jase worked hard to keep his face impassive, clenching his teeth in the process. Now he could see it. The picture Jack had shown him of Tempest Agent Simon Skinner revealed a man with reddish hair, but in full living color, Simon's hair must be a match for this man's. "Nina?"

She huffed out a breath, as if she'd been holding it from the moment she'd confronted this man.

"Th-that's not possible. Simon had no siblings."

One corner of the man's mouth lifted. "That he knew of. Simon told you he'd been adopted, didn't he?"

"Yes." Nina had loosened her grip on Jase's wrist, although the imprint from her fingernails remained.

"That's why I'm a Kitchens, not a Skinner." He held out his hand. "Chris Kitchens."

When nobody moved to shake his hand, Kitchens dropped it. "Our mother gave us up for adoption when I was three and Simon was just a baby. Of course, he'd have no conscious memory of me, but I remembered a baby brother and when I got my stuff together I decided to find him."

Nina clasped her hands in front of her and faced Jase. "Simon Skinner was my ex-fiancé."

Jase nodded. She could interpret that any way she wanted.

Chris continued. "So, you can imagine my disappointment when I went through all the time and trouble to locate my brother only to…not locate him. I found his life to an extent, and I found you, but not much more."

"H-how did you find me?"

"I was able to track down Simon's last known address, which was an apartment in your name. A little more digging by a PI friend of mine led me to Break Island."

"I'm sorry. I can't help you, Chris. Simon and I split up months ago, and I haven't seen him since."

"Yeah, I gathered that from some of your neighbors in LA."

Jase ground his back teeth even more. If Chris and his PI friend had tracked down Nina that easily, what chance did she have against Tempest if that agency wanted to find her?

"And yet you still followed me out to Washington?" Her eyes narrowed and her spine stiffened. "Why?"

Chris shrugged his big shoulders. "I don't know. I thought maybe you'd heard from him. Maybe I just wanted to find out about my baby brother from someone who knew him well. Y-you did know Simon well, didn't you? I mean, you two were engaged."

Nina smiled a tight smile while tucking her hair behind her ear. "Of course."

Jase swallowed. You had to feel for the guy. He'd searched high and low for a brother he remembered before adoption split them apart, and now that brother was dead. And Jace couldn't even tell him. Couldn't tell Nina—not yet anyway.

"Why don't you come back with us?" He pointed to the ferry to Break Island chugging away from the dock. "I think you missed that boat."

"Sure, if—" he glanced at Nina "—if it's okay. I won't stay too long, Nina. Who knows? Maybe after talking to you, I'll be able to find Simon myself."

"Maybe." Nina's flat voice didn't offer much encouragement for that endeavor. "I'm sorry. Chris, this is Jase Buckley."

Jase shook the other man's hand. "I'm staying at the B and B and helping Nina fix up the place."

"I'd offer you a room, but I'm not ready to take on guests yet."

"No problem. I already booked a room at a motel in town." He tapped the cart. "Do you want me to return this for you?"

"Sure." Jase shoved it in his direction. "We'll get the boat ready for takeoff."

When Chris took off with the cart, Nina turned to him. "Sorry about the craziness. He looks a lot like his brother, my ex-fiancé, and I thought…"

"You thought your ex had come back for you?"

"Something like that."

"Is that something you want? I mean, do you want to get back together with Simon?"

She snapped, "No!"

He took her by the shoulders. "Did your ex hurt you, Nina? You were so freaked out about this guy, Chris."

"Simon never physically harmed me, but he could've been heading that way. I have to believe it was PTSD, but he wouldn't get help."

Chris came back into view and Nina grabbed Jase's arm and put her finger to her lips. "Chris doesn't need to know anything like that about his brother, okay? I plan to tell him only the good stuff."

"I think that's a good idea. He's gonna be heartbroken enough as it is."

Nina tilted her head and wrinkled her nose. "What do you mean?"

Jase sealed his lips and busied himself with the motor.

"Why's Chris going to be heartbroken?"

He glanced up at the big redhead barreling toward the dock. "Just that after thinking he'd found his brother, he's gone."

"Yeah, maybe he will have some luck tracking him down." She turned and waved to Chris. "Hop on board."

Jase maneuvered the boat across the water, passing the ferry at the midpoint of the trip. The brisk wind and the rumbling motor on the boat kept conversation to a minimum. All passengers seemed lost in their own thoughts anyway.

He had sized up Chris and felt comfortable enough to invite him back to Break Island with them. He was headed that way anyway, whether or not they'd extended the invitation. This way, Jase could keep an eye on him.

Nina seemed to think Chris resembled Simon enough to believe he was her ex-fiancé, so the story about him and Simon as brothers separated by adoption rang true.

Tempest wouldn't go through the trouble of finding someone who resembled Simon and then sending him out here with that story—would they?

Jase didn't know too much about Tempest. Like his agency, Prospero, Tempest was deep undercover, beneath the umbrella of the CIA but involved in missions completely off the radar.

Even Jack Coburn had only a foggy notion of Tempest's assignments. Jase hadn't given the other agency much thought at all until one of its agents, Max Duvall, had come in with wild stories about superagents and drugs and world chaos.

He gazed at the approaching shoreline of the peaceful island and snorted. Break Island was about as far removed from that world as it could be.

Missing siblings turning up unexpectedly? That, it had in spades.

As the boat eased up to the Kleinschmidts' dock, Chris jumped from the deck and started pulling the craft in.

"You know your way around a boat?" Jase tossed him the anchor rope.

"I should hope so. I spent five years in the navy."

Nina drew in a breath. "Simon was in the navy, too."

"I know that." He looped the end of the rope around the post. "That's how I was able to get some info on him."

With his back to the bay, Chris surveyed the island. "This sure is pretty. Simon spend much time here?"

"None at all. We had a busy life in LA. When he managed to get time off, we'd spend it in Hawaii, mostly."

"One of my favorite places, too." He snapped his fingers. "It's sort of like twins separated at birth, except Simon and I were two years apart."

They got the boat docked, and Chris helped him carry the supplies and groceries to Moonstones. Jase watched Nina closely, wondering if and when she planned to tell Chris he was going to be an uncle.

But so far, her lips were sealed.

Maybe Jack and Prospero had been wrong for once. He didn't doubt that his agency had discovered Nina's pregnancy, but maybe she'd lost the baby.

A knife twisted in his gut and he almost doubled over. He wiped a sudden bead of sweat from his brow with the back of his hand. He had to stop taking this whole assignment so personally. From accessing her medical records, Prospero had no indication that she'd lost the baby.

"You okay?" Chris slapped him on the back after dropping off another load of soil next to the porch.

"Low blood sugar. I haven't eaten in a while."

Nina stood on the porch, hooking her thumbs in the pockets of her jeans. "I think we all need something to eat."

"Is there someplace we can meet for dinner?" Chris

pointed to the bend in the road. "I think I'm headed that way into town. I'll check into my motel and we can meet up later."

"Mandy's. It's on the main street. You can't miss it, or ask a local. Six okay?"

"Fine with me. Thanks, Nina, for humoring me."

"I understand completely. I'm sure it's what Simon would want."

"So, where do you think he is?"

She shrugged. "He had a job with the government. They sent him places, sometimes for a long time."

"Six months?"

"I can't help you with that part of it, Chris."

"I understand. Dinner is enough. I just want to find out everything about my brother, or as much as you can tell me."

Nina joined Jase at the fence to watch Chris follow the road to town.

She murmured under her breath, "No, you don't."

"A few little white lies won't hurt. Then if he ever does find Simon, he can make his own judgments." He smacked the top of the post. "Let's put this stuff away. You can do the groceries, and I'll take care of the yard supplies. Still don't trust a store where you can buy fertilizer along with five-gallon jugs of milk."

Nina disappeared inside the house, and Jase hoisted a bag of soil onto his shoulder and walked to the back of the B and B.

He lifted his work cell phone from the inside zippered pocket of his jacket and placed a call to his boss.

"What do you have to report, Jase?"

Jack knew agents didn't use these phones for social calls.

"A twist."

"Is the subject okay?"

"The subject."

"Ah, Nina Moore."

"The subject's fine, but her ex-fiancé's long-lost brother showed up on her doorstep."

"Simon Skinner doesn't have a brother. He has no family. That's the way Tempest prefers its agents—rootless, alone."

"Skinner was adopted, right?"

"Yeah."

"Well, he had a brother who was adopted out, too. The brother is older and remembered having a younger sibling."

Jack's voice sharpened. "You're sure? Could be a Tempest ploy."

"Don't think so. Apparently, the guy's the spitting image of Simon Skinner."

"Name?"

"Chris Kitchens."

"We'll look into him."

"Nina's flaky sister made an appearance on the island, too."

"This is getting more complicated than we'd bargained for. Keep the players straight and keep the subject safe."

"I'm on it."

"You still think this is an unnecessary babysitting job?"

"I haven't seen any evidence of Tempest's interest in Nina yet."

"I had a gut feeling Tempest wasn't going to ignore Skinner's fiancée, ex or otherwise."

"I know all about your gut feelings, Jack. That's what I'm doing out here."

"It's more than a gut feeling now, Bennett."

Jase's pulse ticked up a notch. "Why is that?"

"Simon Skinner finally turned up—dead."

Chapter Eight

Nina stood on her tiptoes on the chair to shove the package of thirty-six rolls of toilet paper onto the top shelf in the storage room. She didn't need them now, but once guests started checking in on a regular basis, they'd come in handy. They'd probably come in handy once this baby started crowding her bladder, too.

A pair of strong hands clasped her around the hips. "What the hell are you doing?"

She glanced down into Jase's face, lined with worry. "I'm putting away some toilet paper."

"This chair isn't exactly steady, and if you have to go up on your tiptoes, it's not high enough."

"Okay, but it's not like I'm twenty stories high."

He took her hand. "Let me help you down."

She stepped down in front of him, facing him only inches apart. "I can't figure you out."

His dark eyes deepened to inky unfathomable depths. "What's to figure out?"

"Either you grew up with sisters and were very protective of them, or you were in a house full of boys and treated your mother like a queen." She bit the end of her finger to lighten the mood, since she could feel the tension coming off his taut body.

He cracked a smile. "Neither. I have one sister and

we fought like a couple of boxers circling each other in a ring, and everyone else treated my mother like a queen, so I was spared Her Majesty's service."

"Must be a military thing, then."

"Probably." He lifted a shoulder and stepped around her. "I'm going to clean up for dinner."

"You don't have to go, Jase." Would he really want to sit through a litany of Simon's accomplishments and virtues? "I know you have writing to do, and you've gotten precious little of that done since you've arrived on Break Island."

"I think it's a good idea if I tag along."

"Why? Do you suspect Chris of some ulterior motive?"

"Do you?"

"Why would you ask that? He looks very much like Simon. For that reason alone, his story rings true."

"Something about all of this—" his hands framed an imaginary ball "—seems off."

She swept her tongue along her dry bottom lip. "What do you mean, *off*?"

"You're a woman who ended an engagement with a man and then haven't laid eyes on that man for months. When you think you see him, your response isn't curiosity or even anger. It's fear." He put out his hand, palm forward. "Don't even deny it, Nina. I saw you. I held you. You were trembling like a petal in a rainstorm."

"I told you. Simon was suffering from PTSD. He was acting crazy before we split up. It's why we split up. He wouldn't get help, denied anything was wrong."

"Do you think he'll track you down?"

She spun away from him and grabbed the storage room doorjamb. "I'm not sure. When I was in LA, it felt like someone was watching me."

Jase sucked in a noisy breath. "Simon?"

"I don't know. I never saw anyone, could never pick out a face in the crowd, but I felt a presence."

Jase's angular features had sharpened even more. "You never told me this."

"Uh, we met yesterday, Jase. That's not something you generally spring on a stranger. It's bad enough that you got the full force of Hurricane Lou, and now my ex-fiancé's brother has come calling. I'm surprised you haven't run for the hills yet."

"That's serious stuff if you think your ex is stalking you, but why wouldn't he just approach you?"

"I don't know. I told him I wouldn't see him again until he got help. He probably hasn't gotten help."

Jase took a step toward her and threaded his fingers through hers. "It's not Simon."

She whispered, "How do you know that?"

"It just doesn't make sense." He toyed with her fingers. "I don't think he'd creep around stalking you. If anything, he'd confront you head-on. The way you describe him, he sounds like that guy."

Her nose tingled with unspent tears. Jase made her feel so good, so safe. Should she tell him now about her pregnancy? It might be the last straw to send him running for the exit, but she wanted him to know everything. She'd be making the switch to maternity clothes in the next week anyway. Much better to tell him than announce it with a maternity shirt hugging her visible baby bump.

He chucked her beneath the chin with his knuckle. "Let's go meet Chris and give him a glowing report of his brother. It's the least you can do for the guy."

She blinked and nodded, not even trying to recapture the moment between them. Jase was a nice guy, a protective guy—a hot guy—but what did she really owe him? He might find it too intimate for her to tell him about her baby as if it was some kind of special announcement. Better to mention it in an offhand way.

"I'm going to hit the shower. Meet you in the sitting room in about twenty minutes."

She allowed him to escape the storage room without embarrassing him with any more personal revelations.

She showered and shimmied into a pair of black leggings that she topped with an oversize blue sweater that hit the top of her thighs and a pair of black knee-high boots.

When she entered the sitting room, Jase turned from studying pictures on the mantel. "Your mom and stepdad look like a young couple experiencing first love."

"Yeah, and that was taken after they'd been together for ten years."

"Isn't it what every couple aspires to?"

"At the expense of their kids?" She flicked her fingers in the air. "I don't think so. You have to be a family unit first."

"Family units are not all they're cracked up to be." He slipped her keys from the hook in the kitchen. "You ready? I think we should take the truck into town and skip the late-night walk."

"Afraid of running into my crazy sister again?"

"Would you think less of me if I copped to that?"

"I'd think you had your head on straight." She winked at him.

Jase insisted on driving the truck and she let him. He parked half a block from Mandy's.

"Looks like more people in town tonight."

"I think it's the big storm."

"People are heading to the island because of the storm? You'd think they'd want to stay away."

"Once the storm starts blowing full force, there's no fishing. Most of these guys have to get their fix in before the moratorium."

"The storms pretty bad here?"

"They can be. This one's supposed to be coming down from Alaska. It can shut down the island—nothing coming, nothing going."

"Do you have a generator at Moonstones?"

"I don't have a working dishwasher at Moonstones."

"Got it."

Chris was waiting in front of Mandy's like an eager puppy dog. In that way, he resembled Simon not at all. Simon had nothing of the puppy dog about him. He had the intensity of a jungle cat, sort of like Jase.

Chris grinned and pumped their hands. "I like this island—friendly town."

"Where did you say you lived, Chris?" Nina crossed her arms low on her waist, cupping her elbows. She hoped he didn't have any plans to settle here.

"Arizona—going back there once I finish my search for my brother."

Jase got the door and held it open for her and Chris. "You're continuing your search after this?"

"Sure, why not?"

Jase caught her eye as she passed him and raised one eyebrow.

They were seated by the window again, and Jase tapped the menu. "Fish-and-chips two nights in a row?"

"Go for it. Live dangerously. It'll be good for your book."

Chris looked over the top of his menu. "You're writing a book?"

"Trying to."

"What's it about?"

"War story, fictional account."

"Were you in the service?"

"Marines."

"Ah, sorry to hear that." Chris chuckled. "Were you deployed in Iraq or Afghanistan?"

"Two tours of duty in Afghanistan."

"I'd read that book." Chris downed half his water. "From what I got out of the navy, Simon did a couple of tours in Afghanistan and then seemed to drop off the radar—just like now. Makes me wonder what he was into. The navy wouldn't tell me anything more."

"Lotta stories to be told." Jase closed the menu and dropped it to the table. "I have to go with the fish-and-chips again."

Nina took a sip of her own water, eyeing Jase over the rim of the glass. He didn't seem all that eager to talk about Simon. Maybe he should've stayed home to write, because she planned to give Chris a glowing report of his brother to make him that more anxious to find him and send him on his way.

The waitress approached their table and flipped open her pad. "You ready?"

They all ordered the fish-and-chips, and the men ordered beers. Nina stuck to water.

When the waitress left, Chris hunched over the table. "Tell me about Simon. Do you have any pictures?"

Of course she had pictures. After the breakup, her inclination had been to delete all pictures of Simon from her phone. She'd gotten rid of a few, but stopped when she found out about her pregnancy. Her child deserved to know what his father looked like, even if he never saw him or met him.

She pulled her cell from her purse and tapped her photos. She'd moved them all to a separate album. Another tap and Simon's face filled the screen, his megawatt smile and bright red hair causing a lump to form in her throat.

He'd been a good man, full of joy and ridiculous impressions. Why did he change?

She handed the phone to Chris. "That's Simon."

"Wow, we do look alike."

"You can scan through that whole album. All those pictures are of Simon."

Chris's eyes met hers. "You're not one of those exes who trashes and burns every picture? I had one of those. My girlfriend and I split up, got back together a few months later, and I'd come to find out she deleted every image of me off her phone. Then we broke up again. Are you holding on to these because you hope to get back together with Simon someday?"

Nina ignored Jase, even though she could feel his gaze focused on her like a laser beam. Was he jealous? Would she mind if he was?

"Simon and I won't be getting back together, but he was a part of my history and I'm not about to rewrite history."

"I like that attitude. Why'd you two break up, if you don't mind my asking?" Chris thanked the waitress when she placed his beer in front of him and then returned to the pictures on the cell phone.

She shrugged. "We both changed, went our different ways. It was mutual."

As he slid through each image, he peppered her with questions. She answered him with the vision of the old Simon in her head—the cheerful, fearless, protective man she'd fallen in love with, not the paranoid, angry man given over to fits of rage she'd kicked out of their house and her life.

Occasionally, Jase would lean across the table to look at a particular picture, his features sharp as if on high alert. Simon had that look about him at times, too, much more toward the end—always on edge, always expecting something to happen.

She must be drawn to that intense type, because she

had to admit it to herself, pregnant or not, she was drawn to Jase Buckley.

Their platters of deep-fried fish and golden French fries arrived just as Chris had thumbed through the last picture of Simon. He placed the phone next to her plate and patted her hand. "Thanks for that, Nina. Makes me more determined than ever to find my brother."

Jase rubbed his hands together and reached for the vinegar. "Best fish-and-chips I've ever had."

Nina threw a sharp glance in his direction. Way to break a mood.

Chris didn't seem to notice or care as he squeezed a lemon quarter all over his food. "Looks great."

As they dug in to their meals, the conversation turned to fishing and the weather.

"I understand there's a big storm heading down this way." Chris took a sip of beer and the foam clung to his red mustache. "Do you ever get cut off?"

"Cut off, blacked out, flooded—you name it."

"I should probably take off before all that happens."

"Where are you headed next?" Jase ran his fork through a glob of tartar sauce before stabbing a piece of fish.

"I think I'll go back to LA to see if I can pick up any more threads down there. That's the last place I can track him to. I appreciate the pictures and all, Nina, but I was hoping you could tell me where to find him."

"If I knew, I'd tell you." She folded her hands around her glass of water. "We broke it off. He packed up his things, took his car and left. I didn't hear one word from him after that."

"Did you have a big fight at the end? Was he distraught or suicidal?"

She shoved her glass aside. "Look, Chris. Simon was suffering from PTSD. I wasn't going to tell you because I didn't want to concern you, but if you're going to take up this search, you need to know. Simon was going off the rails. He was paranoid. I think he had delusions. People were after him. He was raging against some unseen enemy. I encouraged him to get help, but he refused. The day I gave him the ultimatum is the day he walked out."

Chris whistled. "I'm glad you told me, Nina. Why did you think you had to hide it from me?"

"Because you wanted to know your brother, and that wasn't Simon. Simon was all those things I told you about him."

"You're wrong, Nina. That was a part of Simon, too." Chris shifted his gaze to Jase's face. "Am I right, man? That was a part of him."

Jase nodded. "You're right, but maybe now's not the best time to go searching for him."

"There's no better time." Chris slapped the table. "Thanks for telling me that, Nina. It gives a whole new urgency to my quest."

"Not happy with just one guy, gotta have two?"

Nina groaned and closed her eyes briefly before meeting her sister's watery blue eyes. "I thought you'd be on your way by now, Lou."

"Kip and I are on vacation. We're going to hang out for another day or two, and you know how I love a raging storm." She wagged her finger in Nina's face. "But don't think we've given up on Moonstones. Kip's brother is an attorney in Seattle and he thinks I might have a case against you."

"Kip's brother thinks that or Kip? 'Cause Kip looks pretty out of it right now." She pointed at her sister's shadow swaying behind her.

"Whatever." Lou batted her eyelashes. "Who's this cutie?"

"This is Chris Kitchens. Chris, my sister, Louise Moore, and her friend Kip…"

"Chandler." Kip stuck out a surprisingly steady hand. "You a local?"

Nina held her breath and glanced at Jase.

"Me?" Chris crumpled up his napkin and tossed it onto his empty plate. "Naw, I just came out here to find Nina."

Lou blew a strand of dyed blond hair from her face. "Everyone wants Nina."

"Oh, no, it's not like that. I'm Simon's brother."

Nina was clenching her jaw so tightly her teeth ached.

Lou widened her eyes. "Am I supposed to know who Simon is?"

"Simon Skinner. Nina's ex-fiancé."

"Whoa-ho, girl, you work fast."

"Don't you have a joint to smoke somewhere?" Nina kicked Jase under the table, but she didn't know what she expected him to do. From the look on his face, he didn't know, either.

"What does that mean?" Chris cocked his head and ran a thumb across his mustache.

"This—" Lou poked a finger in Jase's direction "—is Nina's fiancé now, so I don't know how long ago she was engaged to your brother."

Chris's jaw hung open as he turned to Nina, his gaze darting to Jase's face. "Really?"

"Sorry, Chris." Nina pressed her fingers against her hot cheek.

"That's your business, but is what you told me about Simon's PTSD true or did you two break it off because of Jase?"

"Not at all." Jase kicked her back. "I met Nina after the breakup. It just happened fast for us."

"Wish you all the best, then." Chris reached for his wallet. "Let me pay for dinner for all your trouble today."

Jase already had cash out. "We'll get it."

"Tell you what." Chris tapped her phone. "You send

me a few of those pictures of Simon, I'll pick up dinner and we'll call it even."

"I'd be happy to." She shoved her phone across to him. "Call me from your phone so I have the number."

Kip had wandered off to the bar, but Lou hadn't given up yet. Placing a hand on Chris's shoulder, she leaned over the table. "If you want a ride back to the mainland in style, Kip and I can hook you up."

Chris looked up from placing his call to Nina's cell. "Really?"

"If the boats stop running because of this storm, Kip has a line on a helicopter."

Nina raised her eyebrows. "Kip has a helicopter?"

"I don't know about that. It probably belongs to his brother, who's a big-time lawyer. I just know because I heard him on the phone asking around for helipads on the island."

"Thank you, I'll keep your offer in mind."

Disappointed that she hadn't stirred up more trouble, Lou joined Kip at the bar, where he had a beer waiting for her. They drank them down and left before Chris even paid the bill.

When the waitress dropped off the check, Chris studied it and said, "I think they charged us for two more beers. You just had one, right?"

"Yeah."

Chris waved to the waitress. "We just had two beers at this table, and you charged us for four."

She jerked her thumb over her shoulder. "That couple who was at your table earlier? They had a couple of beers at the bar and said you were picking up the tab."

Nina rolled her eyes. "And you didn't think to check with us first?"

"Sorry, hon. They were over here."

"Chris, I'll pay for my sister's drinks."

"That's all right. Some bad blood there?"

Jase snorted. "In case you hadn't noticed, Nina's *step*-sister has some issues."

"I sure hope when Simon and I finally meet, we'll get along. I'll make sure of it."

"Good luck with that, man." He clapped Chris on the shoulder.

Nina grabbed her jacket and scooted out of the booth. If Chris ever found Simon, would he report back to him that she'd gotten engaged? How had everything gotten so complicated? She'd come out to Break Island to escape complication.

Jase opened the door of the restaurant, and as Nina stepped onto the sidewalk, droplets of rain, propelled by the wind, pelted her face. "Looks like we're getting the edge of that storm creeping in."

"You left your umbrella in the restaurant. I'll get it."

As Jase returned to the restaurant, Nina turned to Chris. "Do you plan to stick around the island?"

"Maybe for a day or two, but don't worry. I can look around on my own. You've been helpful and you didn't have to be."

"I just hope you find what you're looking for, Chris, and that you're not disappointed." She reached out to him, feeling guilty and sorry at the same time.

As he hugged her, a piercing screech came from behind. Before Nina had a chance to react, a strong force yanked on the back of her hair, dragging her from Chris's embrace.

She staggered backward, her arms flailing.

"You bitch! You have to take everything. One fiancé. Two fiancés. Are you working on your third?"

As Lou screamed in her ear, she began driving her bony knee into Nina's back.

Nina's feet scrambled on the wet sidewalk to gain

purchase, and then suddenly the threat evaporated. She turned to see Jase lifting Lou off her feet by the back of her jacket.

Lou dangled there like a scarecrow until Jase set her down with a jolt.

"Keep your hands off Nina. She's pregnant."

Chapter Nine

Everyone froze. She still had her hands splayed in front of her to ward off Lou's next attack, but she didn't have to worry.

Lou's feet were rooted to the sidewalk where Jase had dropped her, with her mouth hanging open and a wild look in her eye.

Even Chris stood as still as a statue.

How the hell did Jase know about her pregnancy? And why the hell did he choose to announce it in front of these two particular people?

Chris broke the silence first. "Is it…? Is it…?"

Nina took a shuddering breath. She couldn't handle this—not now. "No, Chris. It's not Simon's. It's the reason Jase and I decided to speed up our commitment."

She finally met Jase's eyes. Poor guy. First she'd foisted an engagement on him and now a baby. Poor guy? Her nostrils flared. How dare he spill the beans like this in the middle of the sidewalk.

Lou sank to the ground, her keening wail putting an end to any conversation. Nina shot a worried look at her stepsister crumpled on the ground, rocking back and forth.

She finally noticed Kip hugging the wall near where Lou must've launched her attack. She swept her arm toward Lou. "Help her. Lou, what's wrong?"

"A baby, a baby, a baby." Lou raised her tear-streaked face, her mascara little black rivulets down her cheeks. "I've always wanted a baby."

Lou's words sent a shower of cold fear down her back. Lou had never expressed any interest in children before. Now she wanted a baby?

Nina pushed a lock of wet hair from her face. "You need help, Lou."

"We're leaving." Jase stepped into the circle that had formed around Lou's forlorn figure. He put an arm around Nina's shoulders and held out his hand to Chris. "I hope you find peace with your brother."

Then he pointed a finger at Kip. "You'd better get her out of here unless you want to see her get locked up for being drunk in public."

Jase steered her down the street, opening the umbrella over their heads.

Nina glanced over her shoulder at both Kip and Chris helping Lou to her feet and Chris draping his jacket over her shoulders. Chris was that kind of guy, just like his brother used to be.

When they got to the truck, Jase helped her in and then blasted the heat when he started the engine. He rested his hands on the steering wheel and stared straight ahead without putting the truck in gear.

"Sorry, you know, sorry I did that."

She folded her hands across her belly. "How did you know I was pregnant?"

His hands tightened around the steering wheel. "I don't know. Little things. You didn't drink alcohol. Your silhouette when you were all wet after I pulled you from the water. You put your hands on your stomach a lot."

"Do I?" She lifted her hands from her stomach and sighed.

"I was waiting for you to tell me. I figured you'd do it

in your own time, or, you know, you don't owe me any explanations or anything."

"But why then?" She watched a droplet of water tremble on the end of a strand of hair and then fall to her thigh. "Why did you have to blurt it out at that moment—in front of Lou, in front of Chris?"

"I don't know." He pressed the heel of his hand against his forehead. "I wanted to stop Lou without physically throwing her against a wall."

"Yeah, well, picking her up by the scruff of the neck did a pretty good job of stopping her."

"She was still moving and squirming. I knew the minute I let her go she'd resume her assault on you."

"Thanks for stepping in, but I wish you hadn't let the cat out of the bag about my pregnancy."

He drummed his thumbs against the steering wheel. "Why didn't you tell Chris it was Simon's? It *is* Simon's, isn't it?"

"Of course he's Simon's."

"You're having a boy?" Jase turned toward her, but his gaze shifted over her shoulder to stare into the wet night.

"Yes, and I didn't want to tell Chris because I didn't want to complicate his life even more than it is. He's so hell-bent on finding Simon and so convinced that he's going to have some wonderful, brotherly reunion, I didn't want to dump this on him, too."

"Are you ever going to tell him?"

She patted her cell phone in her purse. "I have his info. I'll tell him later when everything settles down, and if he wants to be an uncle to the baby, that's fine. He seems like a decent guy."

His eyes locked on to hers. "You're not trying to keep this pregnancy from Simon, are you?"

"God, no. I wouldn't do that. But as you can tell from Chris's fruitless search, Simon is not an easy guy to find.

But if he is stalking me, he needs to get help before I tell him anything."

As always when she started talking about Simon, Jase's face closed down and shutters came down over his eyes. He started the truck. "Why do you think Lou went off like that?"

"Because she's unbalanced, and the way she self-medicates with booze and drugs only makes her worse. She needs a good treatment facility. Dad offered many times to pay for it, but she refused."

He checked the rearview mirror and pulled onto the street. "I think she could be a danger to you and the baby, Nina, and I think you're fooling yourself if you think her stunt with the boat and her attack tonight weren't meant to cause you physical harm."

"You're probably right." She twisted her fingers together and leaned her head against the cool glass of the window. "I came up here to Break Island to get away from the fear and the tension, and it looks like they followed me."

"Do you really think Simon is stalking you?"

She hadn't meant to harp on her suspicions, especially since Jase was taking this protectiveness thing to a whole new level.

"I don't have any reason to believe he is. When we split up, he left—no begging, no threats—it was as if he couldn't care less. I don't know why he would be stalking me, but I can't think of anyone else who would tamper with my car and lie in wait for me in a parking structure."

"What?" He slammed on the brakes in the middle of the road and the truck's back tires fishtailed.

She grabbed the dashboard. "For being an overly protective type, you should learn to drive more carefully."

"Someone tampered with your car? You didn't mention that before."

"I'm not really sure. I had no proof, but my car had been working just fine before that and it sure seemed like there was a car following me."

"When did this happen? Right after Simon left or later?"

"Not right away. It was later, after I discovered I was pregnant. That's why I suspected Simon. I figured maybe he found out about the baby and got some weird notion in his head to start following me around—maybe to see if the baby was his."

"You never saw him?"

"Oh, I saw flashes of red hair here and there." She tugged on her earlobe. "Just like today, only today I matched the hair to a real person. In LA, I was never able to do that. I don't know."

"You don't know what?" He'd continued driving and Moonstones came into view.

"I thought the hormones were making me paranoid. At least here on Break Island, Lou really *is* after me. It's not all in my head."

"Do you believe the feelings you had in LA were all in your head?"

She planted her hands on her knees and hunched forward. "The feelings I had were real. Whether or not those feelings were based on anything real is another story. Does that make sense?"

"Yep."

They dashed through the rain, and when they stepped inside the B and B, Jase hung up the umbrella on a hook by the front door. "I'm going to get that fire going. You go get into some dry clothes, or better yet, some warm pajamas. Do you want some warm milk? Tea?"

"I'll take some tea." She turned at the hallway that led to the back of the house. "Are you always this bossy, Jase Buckley?"

"This is nothing."

She disappeared into the back, and Jase strode to the fireplace and prodded the charred wood from yesterday's fire. He hoisted a few more pieces onto the grate and tucked some kindling into the spaces.

In two minutes, he had the flames dancing across the wood and he stared into the flickers of orange and gold. How could he have been so stupid?

Straight up, he wouldn't be able to tell if a woman was pregnant any more than he'd be able to tell what she ate for dinner. He must've bluffed his way through that one, because she seemed to believe his line of bull.

If the boss could've seen his performance tonight out on that sidewalk, Coburn would've questioned his sanity.

Nina had been faster on her feet than he'd been, telling Chris that Simon wasn't the father. All he needed was for Chris Kitchens to be hanging around Nina, bringing up Simon every other minute.

Man, he felt for the guy. Waiting all this time to track down his brother only months after that brother had died. Once Prospero and the CIA could straighten things out regarding Simon Skinner's story, they'd have to notify Chris…and Nina.

Maybe he'd be long gone by then, out of Nina's life.

Had she been right about her suspicions in LA? She might believe it was Simon who'd been stalking her, but he knew that couldn't be true. Prospero had finally confirmed Max Duvall's story, and even if they never recovered Simon's body, they had no reason to doubt that Duvall had killed him in self-defense. But if not Simon, who?

Would her stepsister have gone down to LA to watch Nina? Stalking didn't seem to be Lou's style. She preferred an all-out, in-your-face attack.

Could the boss be right again? Had Tempest already

been following Nina in LA? For what purpose? She knew
nothing about Simon's work.

"You're hogging all the warmth."

Still crouching in front of the fireplace and a now-
blazing fire, he cranked his head around. Nina had
wrapped herself in a pink robe that matched her cheeks.
She'd dried her hair and it floated around her shoulders
like a cloud.

"The flames can be hypnotic." He rose to his feet and
stretched. "And I didn't make your tea."

"I can make my own tea."

"Sit." He pointed to the chair across from the fireplace.
"I'm bossy, remember?"

"It's sweet of you to be so concerned, but I'm not going
to break."

"Sweet?" He scratched his jaw. "That's the first time
that adjective's ever been used to describe me."

"Oh, please." She settled into the chair and curled her
long legs beneath her. "You're probably great with your
nieces and nephews, too."

"Nieces and nephews? That's a laugh. My sister's the
type who would eat her young." He crossed into the kitchen
and started filling the kettle with water.

"Really? I'm surprised."

"You don't know my sister."

"No, I mean I'm surprised you're not an uncle. I
would've thought the way you picked up on my pregnancy, you'd been around a pregnant woman before. I
just assumed your sister…"

He swore under his breath. He was getting himself in
deeper and deeper here. He had to stop acting so natural
around Nina. This wasn't natural.

He wasn't writing a book. He didn't need to work as
a handyman to make money. He hadn't recognized any
signs that she was pregnant. His agency had spied on her.

"A lot of my buddies have been getting married lately and having kids. Seems like a new baby popped out every other month."

He folded his arms and leaned against the counter that separated the kitchen from the sitting room.

"I suppose these things do run in cycles." She held her hands out to the fire. "You're sure you're not married with five children at home?"

He forced a laugh and then gratefully turned toward the whistling kettle. "Seven."

"Seven what?"

"Kids."

She laughed, but it was a tight, mirthless sound. She doubted him.

He had to come clean, had to tell her about Simon—at least the part where he was dead. Coburn had wanted to verify Simon's death and parts of Max Duvall's story before releasing any information to Simon's loved ones. Nina still counted as a loved one, since Simon was the father of the baby she was carrying.

Poor little thing—no daddy from the get-go.

He poured the hot water over the tea bag and carried the cup to her, still curled up in the oversize chair.

She thanked him and winked. "You're not joining me this time?"

"I discovered I don't like hot tea."

"I have cold beer in the fridge."

"After the day I had, I'm going to take you up on that offer." He returned to the kitchen and peered into the fridge at three bottles lined up on the shelf. "Are these all local breweries?"

"I have three cases in the storage room and put one of each type in the fridge, just in case. They're all good."

He grabbed a pale ale with an interesting label and used

a bottle opener to pop the top. He settled into the love seat closest to hers, just like last night.

Only everything between them had changed.

"Don't you think it would've been a better idea to have this baby in your home city with your friends around?"

"I have friends here—a different type of friend, people who knew my parents, women who cooked for my dad during Mom's illness—the type of friend that will be here for me when the time comes."

"You don't have those kinds of friends in LA?"

"I have good friends there, friends to lunch with, meet at coffeehouses, attend concerts with, but not the kind to watch a baby in a pinch or know how to put together a crib or who know a home remedy for colic." She blew on her tea and sipped it. "Those people are here, and I need those people around me now."

"I'm sorry…sorry Simon's not in the picture."

"I'm not." She uncurled her legs and wiggled her toes. "Not the way he was acting. I didn't need another unhinged person in my life—Lou is more than enough."

"That's for sure." He whistled between his teeth. "I couldn't believe it when I saw her take a flying leap at you. I still think you could've taken her down, pregnant or not, if she hadn't surprised you."

She rolled her eyes. "Thanks for the vote of confidence, but I'm not going to get into a brawl with my stepsister in the middle of the street."

"It makes sense that you kicked Simon out so quickly after what you've had to deal with in your own family."

She sucked in some tea and then choked on it. "I didn't kick Simon out all that quickly. I encouraged him to get help. I called a psychologist friend of mine. I called the Department of Veterans Affairs."

"What was he doing? What was he saying?"

"He'd come home from an assignment—" she circled

her finger in the air "—he traveled a lot. Worked for the government but couldn't talk about his job much. When he'd get home, he'd lock all the doors and draw the blinds. Sometimes he'd sit for days in front of the TV with a gun in his hand."

"You didn't feel threatened?"

"Not then. His anger and paranoia weren't addressed at me. He kept saying we weren't safe, that if they found out about him, they'd come and get him."

"Did he ever identify who *they* were?" He rubbed the stubble on his chin. This account sounded similar to the types of things Max Duvall had been claiming.

"He never got into it, wouldn't answer me." Hugging herself, she continued. "Then the ranting started alternating with the violence. He'd punch holes in the wall or kick a piece of furniture to pieces."

"That must've been scary, even if it wasn't aimed at you."

"That's the thing." She clasped her hands between her knees. "The last time he was home, he started going on and on about how I was next, how they wouldn't leave me alone, either."

Did Simon Skinner's ranting hold more truth than paranoia? "And that was the final straw?"

"It freaked me out. I still had no idea who he was talking about. Maybe he was talking about himself. I'd been bugging him for weeks to get help, but he refused. When I gave him an ultimatum—get help or leave—he left."

"Would you have made good on your threat?"

"I'd like to think so, but the final punch to the gut was his warning to me never to look him up or contact him again."

"You respected his wishes?"

"About not contacting him?"

"Yeah."

"Up until the time I found out I was pregnant. Then I did everything in my power to find him to tell him, even though I wasn't sure what kind of role he'd play in the baby's life."

"That makes sense."

"Not a whole lot made sense at that time, but I sort of have a theory about how it all went down."

"I'm listening."

He wasn't kidding. Jase had scooted to the edge of the deep chair, bracing his forearms against his knees and hunching forward. He'd been absorbing every detail of her story from the beginning. How was this guy even still single?

"I think Simon found out I was looking for him and why. He knew I wouldn't let him be a father to the baby unless he checked into a treatment facility or went to the VA. Not being ready for that or even believing he needed that, he decided to stalk me instead. Until yesterday when I spotted Chris Kitchens, I figured Simon had given up when I came out here. It's kind of hard to hide on a small island like this."

Jase had covered his face with his hands, digging the tips of his fingers into his thick brown hair.

"What? Do you think that's far-fetched?"

He parted his fingers and peered at her through the spaces. "I don't know, Nina. I think you should try to put Simon out of your mind right now. Concentrate on staying relaxed and happy. That's what you're here for, right? And I'm here to write and help you get this place in working order."

She rolled her shoulders back and slumped in the chair. "You're right. Simon's going to come back or he's not. Maybe Chris will have better luck."

Jase sat back and wrapped his long fingers around his

sweating bottle. He tipped the rest of the contents down his throat. "That's good stuff."

"Do you want another?"

"I'm tired enough as it is. I worked all morning on the fence, fetched you, your groceries and a total stranger who turned your world upside down, fought off a wild Tasmanian devil and let a huge cat out of the bag. I'm ready to hit the sack."

She raised her arms above her head and yawned. "When you put it that way, but you need to promise me something, Jase Buckley."

"Anything." He rose from the chair, beer bottle in hand, and then swooped down to sweep up her cup.

"You need to promise me you'll do some writing tomorrow." She pushed up from the chair and hugged the robe around her body. "I feel so guilty. You came to Break Island to write and you've been entangled in my family drama."

As he turned toward the kitchen, he shrugged. "Family drama's good for my writing."

She paused at the hallway leading back to her living area. "Thanks, Jase, for being there, for everything."

She didn't know if he heard her or not, since his only answer was the clinking of glass. She took a breath to repeat herself and then blew it out as she walked down the hallway. She could add modesty to his list of virtues.

Hours later Nina woke with a start. The rain had increased through the night and drops of it pelted her window in a relentless rhythm.

She rolled to her side and squished down a pillow to see the floating green digits of the alarm clock. Three o'clock?

Groaning, she pulled the pillow over her head. Ever since her pregnancy, once she woke up like this in the early morning hours she'd had a hard time getting back to sleep.

She closed her eyes and tried some deep breathing. A gust of wind hurried the spatters of rain against her window and then blew an errant branch against the pane, where it scratched and tapped out its own Morse code.

Its message was insistent and sinister.

She bolted upright. Sinister?

With her heart pounding, she rolled from the bed and pressed her nose against the window, where trickles of rain formed a pattern on the glass. The window looked out on the deck with the fire pit, and she felt a strong force beckoning her outside.

The deck had been her parents' favorite spot. Her mother had died on that deck, wrapped in blankets and her husband's loving arms. Not wanting to defile the sanctity of the place, her stepfather had shot himself out on the water, but his presence lingered on the deck, just as her mother's did.

She shoved her feet into her clogs and dragged her robe around her body. She made a stop at her closet to retrieve Dad's shotgun—not the weapon he'd used to commit suicide—and shuffled to the front door.

Raindrops sprinkled her face, and she wiped them away as she stepped onto the porch. The clouds parted just long enough for the moon to glisten against the wet leaves before hiding it from view again and casting the ground into darkness.

Nina took the two porch steps slowly and scuffled along the gravel path that led to the side of Moonstones and the deck.

Darkness draped every inch of it. And then a burst of wind picked up the leaves on the ground and sent them dancing in the air and snatched at her robe, daring her to dance with the leaves.

The wind also shoved the clouds apart, and the moon cast a glow over the deck and the fire pit.

A formless shape huddled in one of the chairs and a shaft of fear pierced her heart. She whispered, "Mom?"

Her feet propelled her toward the deck, the clogs slogging through the mud and the hem of her robe dragging behind her.

She gripped the battered wooden railing as she navigated the three steps up to the deck. The clouds decided to play peekaboo with the moon again and bathed the deck in gloom.

She froze, afraid to take a step onto the deck with its rotten spots. As if sensing her hesitation, the wind gently swirled around her and the clouds shifted. The moon spilled its light once more on the deck and Nina picked her way across to the rattan love seat beneath her bedroom window.

She crouched beside the love seat and reached for the pile of clothing in front of her. Her fingers met flesh— cold, dead flesh.

Chapter Ten

The scream that shattered the night launched Jase from the porch. When he hit the ground, he grabbed a handful of leaves on a bush to keep from sliding into the mud. The scream had come from the side of the house, and he aimed his flashlight in that direction and followed the beam of light.

He swept the flashlight up the deck and zeroed in on Nina hunched over a piece of furniture against the wall of the house.

"Nina! Nina, are you okay?"

A pale oval turned his way, and he clambered up the steps of the deck and rushed to her side. His flashlight played over the figure slumped sideways on the love seat and lit up the face of Nina's stepsister, Lou.

Nina craned her head around to look at him, the rain mingling with the tears streaming down her face.

He set down his flashlight, away from the sad spectacle on the love seat, and hooked his hands beneath Nina's arms. "Let's go inside and call 9-1-1."

"She's dead, isn't she?"

She sure looked dead to him, and he'd seen plenty of dead people, but he pressed two fingers against the pulse in her throat to satisfy Nina. "She's gone."

"I don't… Can you see…? Is she hurt?"

"It's too hard to see anything out here, Nina. Let's allow the professionals to do their jobs." He put an arm around her. "You're shivering."

He led her back into the B and B, the flashlight showing them the way. After settling her before the fireplace, he picked up her landline and punched in 9-1-1 to report finding Lou's body.

Then he sat on the arm of Nina's chair and rubbed her back. "Do you want to get out of this wet robe? The hem's all muddy."

She untied the sash and he peeled the robe from her shoulders. She'd been wet and shivering three times in two days. That couldn't be good for the baby.

He put some water on to boil and went into his room to yank the blanket from his bed. When he returned, Nina was rocking back and forth with her hands pinned between her knees.

Dropping the blanket around her shoulders, he said, "Get warmed up. I'll bring you some tea."

When she didn't make a move, he tucked the blanket around her body, noticing for the first time a fullness to her breasts and a rounded belly beneath the filmy material of her nightgown. His desire for her surged through his veins with red-hot need and he dropped the corner of the blanket in her lap, as if it had burned his fingers.

He backed away from her and moved into the kitchen to watch the kettle on the stove. He was losing it. He'd allowed his past disappointments to get mixed up in his feelings for Nina and his job assignment. He had to pull out of this nosedive.

A revolving light from the front of the B and B splashed red light into the sitting room. "Let me do this."

Jase moved to the door, but Nina followed him, the blanket trailing behind her.

He stepped onto the porch as the EMTs were hopping

from the ambulance. He pointed to the side of the house. "She's on the deck."

Two police cars rolled up, facing the B and B, and illuminated the entire yard with white spotlights.

Two police officers approached them. The taller one spoke first. "You're Nina Moore, aren't you? Bruce and Lori's daughter? I'm Sergeant Pruitt."

"Yes, the…the body we found is my stepsister, Louise Moore." She touched Jase's arm. "This is Jase Buckley."

"Good to meet you." The sergeant nodded. "I knew Lou. She caused a bit of ruckus a few nights ago."

"Lou could do that."

"Your father did all he could for that girl." He jerked his head to the side of the house. "What happened?"

Jase answered. "We're not sure. We didn't see any visible signs of injury on the body, but it was dark."

"The body just appeared? No noises? Signs of struggle? How'd you come to find her?"

Nina tugged the blanket closed. "I woke up, and I had a bad feeling. I looked outside first but didn't see anything. Then I walked outside and found her there. I…I must've screamed, because Jase appeared almost immediately after I found Lou."

"You did scream, but I was already coming out here. I heard noises—must've been you coming outside."

"You didn't see anyone else, Ms. Moore?"

"You can call me Nina. I didn't see anyone or anything."

"Did you hear any cars or dogs barking?"

"Just the wind and the ocean, Sergeant Pruitt."

"Yep. Helluva storm coming in." The sergeant used his powerful flashlight to light a path to the deck on the side of the house.

As Nina started to follow him, Jase grabbed her hand. "Why don't you go back inside?"

"She's my sister." She shook him off and caught up to Sergeant Pruitt.

The EMTs had moved Lou's body to a gurney, while the other officer was blocking off the deck with yellow tape.

Jase squinted against the bright light. "What does it look like?"

One of the EMTs answered. "At first look, a drug overdose."

Nina gasped and drove a fist against her mouth.

Jase put his arm around her shoulders and pulled her close. "No signs of violence?"

"Not that we can tell, but we'll deliver the body to the local hospital and the coroner will want to do an autopsy."

Nina choked. "I don't understand how she got here. We left her in town earlier tonight, or rather last night."

The sergeant lifted his shoulders. "It's not a long walk."

"But if she was under the influence or drugged out…"

"Maybe the drugs didn't take full effect until she got here. We'll let the coroner figure that out, Nina, but we need to treat this as a crime scene until we know what happened."

"What does that mean?" She shivered but this time she moved in against Jase instead of pulling away.

His body reacted in all the wrong ways to the feeling of her soft curves melding against his frame.

"Just the deck. When it gets light, the crime scene investigators will come out and survey the area." The sergeant stomped his feet and rubbed his hands together. "Was she with anyone last night when you saw her?"

"Her constant companion on the island, Kip Chandler."

"Oh, yeah, I've seen him around, too."

Jase cleared his throat. "And Chris Kitchens."

"That name I don't know."

Nina tilted her head back to look Jase in the face. "She wasn't really with Chris."

"He was giving her his jacket when we left them."

"Who is this Chris Kitchens?" Pruitt took a pad of paper out of his front pocket.

"He was a visitor to the island. He was looking for his brother, someone I used to know. I couldn't help him with his brother, but we had dinner with him."

"Did he know Lou?"

"He had just met her. He was giving her his jacket because…because it had started raining."

"That's the last you saw of them? Of your stepsister?"

"Yes." Nina turned her face into Jase's arm, pressing her nose against his sweatshirt.

"Sergeant Pruitt, can we finish this inside? Nina's chilled to the bone."

"I think I'm done with my questions tonight." He lifted the tape flapping in the wind. "Stay off the deck until the crime scene techs do their investigation. I'm leaving Officer Jamison here until dawn, which—" he yanked up the sleeve of his jacket "—will be just a few hours from now."

"If you need anything else, Sergeant Pruitt, we'll both be here."

Pruitt's eyes darted from Jase's face to Nina's. "You taking in guests already?"

"Jase isn't really a guest. He's helping me fix up the place in exchange for room and board."

"You *should* fix up this place, Nina. It meant a lot to your mom and stepdad."

"Maybe that's why Lou made her way back here." Her bottom lip trembled along with her voice, and Jase gripped her arm and steered her back toward the house.

"Let us know if you need anything, Sergeant."

"It won't be until sunup, so try to get some rest. "I'm sorry for your loss, Nina."

Jase bundled her back into the B and B while the EMTs and officers were still talking over the body covered by a sheet.

"Get back to bed. I'll get the lights."

She flopped back into the chair and kicked her feet up on the ottoman. "I can't go back to sleep. Lou's still out there."

"What made you get up?"

"I don't know. I felt her presence out there. My mom died on that deck, too."

"Maybe you heard a noise that woke you up."

"That's the logical explanation, isn't it? But nothing about Lou has ever been logical. I thought she was off the hard stuff. I know she was still smoking weed, and she was an alcoholic."

"Maybe it was the booze—alcohol poisoning."

"The EMT thought it was a drug overdose."

"He guessed at that by looking at her in the dark. We'll have to wait for the autopsy."

"Maybe in the end, she was coming to me for help. When she was clearheaded, she could be so funny and warm."

"I wouldn't know. I only ever saw her as an acute danger to you."

Sighing, she rested her head against the chair's cushion. "I suppose I had been waiting for this ending for a while."

"You're still shivering." He nudged her. "Is there room in that chair for me? You need to get warm."

Her eyes widened but she scooted over and he wedged himself into the chair next to her. He repositioned himself and opened his arms so she could rest against his chest. He tugged the blanket around her more closely and she draped her legs over his thighs, burrowing halfway onto his lap.

He held her, and she nestled her cheek against his chest—right above his pounding heart.

He stroked her hair and whispered, "I'm sorry."

Her eyelashes fluttered and her lips parted as if she were ready to answer, but she emitted a soft breath instead.

He tightened his arms around her, and she drifted to sleep. He could hold her for the rest of the morning and never grow tired of watching her face, peaceful and free from worry.

Would Coburn have sent him on this assignment if he'd known the complications of Nina Moore's life? Probably. Some of those complications, namely Chris Kitchens, had deep roots in Nina's connection to Simon Skinner and Tempest.

But she knew nothing of her ex-fiancé's job and life. Tempest had to realize that, too.

He'd step back when the assignment ended. Once they figured out Tempest had no interest in Nina, he'd move on to the next assignment and she could run her B and B and raise her baby—alone.

Lots of women chose single motherhood. Hell, Maggie had insisted on it and Nina had a lot more strength than Maggie did.

After two hours of thinking too much and sleeping too little, Jase shifted his position in the chair as the gray light of dawn seeped through the drapes.

A vehicle pulled up to the house, its engine idling. Must be the crime scene guys relieving the cop standing guard at the deck.

Jase stretched his legs in front of him and slipped his arm from beneath Nina's body. She mumbled and her eyelashes fluttered against her cheeks. He repositioned her head against the cushion of the chair and sauntered to the window to peer outside.

A black van had pulled up in front of Moonstones, discharging personnel from the sliding door on the side where he could make out white letters announcing the Snohomish County Sheriff's Department.

He glanced over his shoulder at Nina, still sleeping, and pulled last night's sweatshirt over his head. Stepping out onto the porch, he walked into beads of moisture that clung to his hair. The clouds from last night continued to threaten, but the storm hadn't rolled in with its full force yet.

One of the techs from the van stopped and waved. "We're here to sift through the location where the body was found, even though the report I saw details a simple overdose."

"Are overdoses ever simple?" Jase shoved his hands into his pockets and walked down the steps.

"Suppose not. Sorry, was she a relative? A friend?"

"My friend's stepsister. She had a lot of problems, so her ending isn't a surprise."

"Still tough to deal with."

The officer from last night emerged from the side of the house, shrugging out of his poncho. "Was Ms. Moore okay last night?"

"She slept. Do you know when the coroner's office is going to release the body for burial?"

He pointed to the techs. "If these guys don't discover anything and the autopsy doesn't indicate foul play, I don't think it'll be that long. But with the storm coming?" He shrugged. "I'm sure the coroner will want to do a toxicology test, and that can take a while out here."

"Did you find anything?"

Jase turned at the sound of Nina's voice. She'd not only woken up, but she'd pulled on a pair of black leggings paired with some fuzzy boots and a down jacket that hung almost to her knees.

"We're just getting started." The lead crime scene tech

patted the black bag slung over his shoulder. "She was your stepsister?"

"Yes. Will you be able to tell how long she'd been on the deck? How long she'd been dead?"

"The autopsy will get to that. We'll look at how she got here and if there was anyone with her."

She blew on her hands and rubbed them together. "I just have a feeling she came here to see me. Maybe she knew she was dying and she wanted to tell me something."

"Between us and the coroner, we should be able to paint a picture of her last hours. I hope it gives you some closure." He joined his team on the deck.

Jase rubbed Nina's arms through the slick, puffy sleeves of her jacket. "How are you feeling?"

"I'm okay. How are you after sleeping upright in a chair all night?" She shook her finger in his face. "Don't think I don't know what you did, Jase Buckley. You watched over me in that chair when you should've just carried me to my bed and gotten a few hours of shut-eye in your own bed."

"You needed to warm up and…"

"Moonstones *does* have central heating."

"…and you needed someone to hold you."

A rush of color stained her cheeks and she twisted her ponytail around her hand. "Did you think I was falling apart?"

"Nina, you'd just found your stepsister's body, hours after she attacked you in the street. Pregnant or not, that's enough to drive anyone to the edge."

She scuffed the toe of her boot against the soft ground. "Thanks for being there. I actually fell asleep and slept through the morning, when I never thought that was going to happen."

"I owe you. You opened your B and B to me without a moment's hesitation."

"Be honest, Jase. I've been nothing but trouble for you ever since you arrived on the island."

She'd spiced up what could've been a boring assignment. He should be thanking her, but that wouldn't play.

"Like I said before, human drama is good for my writing."

"That's putting a good spin on the situation." She took a few steps toward the porch. "I'm going to stop by my sister's room at the motel after breakfast and collect her things and probably pay her bill. I also want to talk to Kip and Chris to find out what they know about last night."

"I'm sure Sergeant Pruitt is already on that."

"I'm sure he is, but that's not going to stop me from talking to those two myself."

"I'll go with you."

She kicked the porch step. "You don't need to do that, Jase. You should be here writing."

"I'm not letting you talk to a guy like Kip by yourself, especially if it gets confrontational. Besides, I write better at night than during the day."

"You're not getting any time at night, either."

"Let me worry about the book, Nina."

"Okay, at least let me cook you breakfast. Blueberry pancakes this morning. Dora Kleinschmidt from next door dropped off some fresh blueberries."

"Fresh blueberries? You don't have to twist my arm." He sprang up the steps past her and held the door open. "I'm going to take a shower and change, and then I'm going to eat pancakes."

He needed to start writing something before Nina got any more suspicious—either that or come clean.

Once he did that, any connection between them would fizzle and die. And he wasn't ready for that.

About an hour and a half later, his belly full of the best damned blueberry pancakes he'd had since his family's

French chef had quit in a huff, he drove Nina in her truck into town and pulled up in front of the police station.

"I hope they can tell me something." She grabbed the handle of the door before the truck even came to a stop.

"Don't get your hopes up. It's been less than twenty-four hours. The crime scene investigators just finished up minutes before we left, and I'm sure the coroner hasn't even started the autopsy yet."

"Okay, you just threw cold water on all my expectations."

He met her at the station door and opened it for her, gesturing her through. The small station had an old-fashioned feel with a counter in the front and enclosed offices beyond that. Vinyl furniture dotted the waiting room.

The officer at the counter glanced up when they walked in, and then her eyebrows jumped to her hairline. "You're Nina Moore, aren't you?"

"Yes. I remember you."

"Nancy Yallop. I used to work patrol when you and your mom first moved to the island." She shook her head. "Such a shame about Louise. Bruce was always worried she'd meet some fate like that."

"I know he was."

"Are you going to call her mother, Inez?"

"I'm hoping to find her number among Lou's stuff." Nina tapped the counter. "Is Sergeant Pruitt in? I know it's early, but I thought he might have some news about Lou."

"Sarge isn't in, but the chief is, and I'm sure he'd like to talk to you." She flicked her fingers at the waiting room. "You can have a seat, but I don't think he's going to be that long."

Officer Yallop disappeared into one of the offices in the back and returned with a smile. "The chief will be out in a minute. Coffee?"

"No, thanks." Nina turned to face him. "Do you want another cup?"

"I'm fine."

"You definitely want to stay away from caffeine. I cut it out for both of mine just to be on the safe side," Officer Yallop said.

Nina spun around, folding her arms over her middle. She'd shed her jacket when they walked into the overheated station. She still sported a pair of black leggings, but her red sweater hugged her body, outlining a distinct baby bump.

Officer Yallop said, "I...I'm sorry. You *are* pregnant, aren't you?"

"I am, but I've just started showing recently, so I'm not used to the attention yet."

"Whew." The officer wiped the back of her hand across her brow. "For a minute there I thought it was foot-in-mouth time, but you're so slim otherwise I didn't think I was mistaken."

The chief came out from the back, bouncing on his toes with each step. His gait could be compensation for his short stature, but what the chief lacked in height he made up in muscle.

"Ms. Moore? I'm Chief Hazlett. Sorry for your loss. I came to the island after your stepfather...passed away, but I did hear some stories about Louise Moore."

"Nice to meet you, Chief. This is Jase Buckley." She extended her hand over the counter. "My stepsister was very troubled."

The chief shook hands with Jase, too, and invited them behind the counter. "Let's talk about this further in my office, although I don't have much to tell you yet."

Nina's shoulders slumped as she followed the chief toward the back of the building, and Jase rubbed the space between her shoulder blades.

"Have a seat." He pointed to two leather chairs across from his desk. The chief's office obviously got the bulk of the furniture allowance in this place.

The chief proceeded to tell them a whole bunch of nothing about the case, except that they didn't find any evidence of foul play—no wounds on Lou's body, no evidence that she'd been dumped on the deck by another party. They'd have to wait for the toxicology report for more details regarding the substances and their quantity in her body.

"What about her companions from last night?" Nina had folded her hands in her lap and her white knuckles stood out against the black of her leggings.

"Can't locate either one of them."

Nina shot a look at Jase, her mouth forming an O. "What does that mean? I told Sergeant Pruitt last night they were all staying in the same motel—The Sandpiper."

"We got that info and even checked out her room, but the men aren't there now."

Jase hunched forward. "The two men checked out?"

"Kitchens did an automated checkout from the TV in the room around midnight and the other guy—" he checked his notes "—Kip Chandler, didn't bother checking out, but the room was in Lou's name. Chandler wasn't at the motel this morning."

Nina perched on the edge of the chair. "I'm going to head over there now and pack up Lou's things and probably settle her bill."

The chief waited until Nina stood up before pushing back from his desk and extending his hand. "We'll keep you posted on your stepsister's autopsy, Ms. Moore, but right now it looks like an unfortunate overdose."

"Of what?" She planted her hands on his desk and leaned forward. "Can they tell yet?"

"Probably heroin."

Nina crossed her hands over her heart and Jase placed a hand on her back.

"I really thought she'd kicked that stuff."

"Once it has you in its grip—" the chief shrugged "—it's a tough monkey to shake."

Jase shook the chief's hand and guided Nina out of his office. They waved to Officer Yallop and landed on the sidewalk in front of the station.

"That's so odd." Nina worried her bottom lip between her teeth. "Didn't Chris say he was going to stick around the island for a day or two?"

"Maybe he decided to get out before the storm hit. He seemed kind of worried about it."

"Kip was Lou's shadow. Why would he disappear?"

"That one's easier." Jase fished the keys to the truck from his pocket. "He was shooting up with Lou, found out what happened and took off."

"Maybe we'll find some answers at The Sandpiper." She waved her phone in the air. "And I'm going to call Chris to find out what happened after we left last night and see if he knows about Lou."

He opened the passenger side of the truck for her, and by the time he climbed into the driver's seat, she was on her cell phone.

She started speaking. "Hi, Chris. This is Nina Moore. I was wondering if you'd heard about my stepsister before you left the island. She OD'd early this morning and passed away. I wanted to find out what went down last night after Jase and I left. Give me a call when you get a chance."

He pulled away from the curb. "If he checked out of The Sandpiper at midnight and left the island, how would he know about Lou?"

"Maybe he heard something from a local. If he's off the island, he got a private boat to take him to the main-

Send For
2 FREE BOOKS
Today!

I accept your offer!

Please send me two
free novels and two mystery
gifts (gifts worth about $10).
I understand that these books
are completely free—even
the shipping and handling will
be paid—and I am under no
obligation to purchase anything,
ever, as explained on the back
of this card.

❏ I prefer the regular-print edition
182/382 HDL GJCE

❏ I prefer the larger-print edition
199/399 HDL GJCE

Please Print

FIRST NAME

LAST NAME

ADDRESS

APT.#   CITY

STATE/PROV.   ZIP/POSTAL CODE

Visit us online at
www.ReaderService.com

Offer limited to one per household and not applicable to series that subscriber is currently receiving.
Your Privacy—The Reader Service is committed to protecting your privacy. Our Privacy Policy is available
online at www.ReaderService.com or upon request from the Reader Service. We make a portion of our mailing
list available to reputable third parties that offer products we believe may interest you. If you prefer that we not
exchange your name with third parties, or if you wish to clarify or modify your communication preferences, please
visit us at www.ReaderService.com/consumerschoice or write to us at Reader Service Preference Service, P.O. Box
9062, Buffalo, NY 14240-9062. Include your complete name and address.

I-815-GF15

▲ Detach card and mail today. No stamp needed. ▲ © 2015 HARLEQUIN ENTERPRISES LIMITED ® and ™ are trademarks owned and used by the trademark owner and/or its licensee. Printed in the U.S.A.

Send For
2 FREE BOOKS
Today!

I accept your offer!

Please send me two
free novels and two mystery
gifts (gifts worth about $10).
I understand that these books
are completely free—even
the shipping and handling will
be paid—and I am under no
obligation to purchase anything,
ever, as explained on the back
of this card.

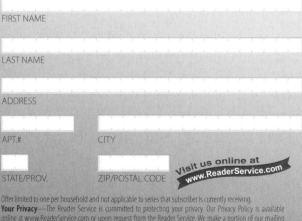

❏ I prefer the regular-print edition
182/382 HDL GJCE

❏ I prefer the larger-print edition
199/399 HDL GJCE

Please Print

FIRST NAME

LAST NAME

ADDRESS

APT.#   CITY

STATE/PROV.   ZIP/POSTAL CODE

Visit us online at
www.ReaderService.com

I-815-GF15

land, because the ferries don't start running until five in the morning."

"That didn't occur to me. Why would he check out of his motel at midnight if there was no place for him to go?"

"Like I said, maybe he made arrangements for a private party to take him across. Lots of people on the island make extra money by ferrying people across."

He drove the short mile to The Sandpiper and swung into a parking space in front of the office.

As soon as they walked in, the motel's manager came from behind the counter. "I was so sorry to hear about Lou, Nina. That girl had her problems, didn't she?"

"She did, Maisie. I know she owed you for the room, so I'll take care of that."

"Well, I don't know how things work when someone's, uh, deceased, but Lou put the room on a credit card. I was just going to charge the card."

"Lou had a credit card? I'll figure it out with her mother, then…when I track her down."

"Good luck with that." She held up her index finger. "I'll get you a key card for the room. Housekeeping hasn't been in there yet since the cops left."

Jase cleared his throat. "You haven't seen Lou's friend, have you?"

"The skinny guy with the shaggy blond hair?" Maisie wrinkled her nose. "No. The cops, Gus Pruitt, already asked me about him. When Gus came by to tell me the news about Lou, we went to the room together, but Kip had cleared out already."

Maisie slid a card across the counter toward Nina, and Nina peeled it from the Formica top. "Thanks, Maisie."

They found Lou's room and Nina slid the card into the slot. She hesitated at the threshold.

"Let me." He stepped around her and pushed open the door.

The smell of stale pizza and cigarettes permeated the room, and he propped open the door so they could breathe. "I guess they ignored the no-smoking rule."

"Lou ignored a lot of rules." Nina moved into the room with folded arms and hunched shoulders as if expecting to find another dead body.

She nudged a pizza box on the floor with the toe of her boot. "I suppose I'll start with the bathroom."

Jase picked up one of the boxes they'd thrown in the back of the truck. "Let me get the stuff from the bathroom and you can pack up her clothes."

"I don't think she ever unpacked." She pointed to an open suitcase in the corner of the room, its contents spilling over the sides.

"Check the drawers and closet, just in case." He left her to Lou's clothes and stepped into the bathroom. It reeked of cigarettes and the slightly sweet smell of marijuana.

Did the two of them think they could hide their drug use by holing up in the bathroom? Maybe this is where they shot up, too.

He kicked at two towels bunched up on the floor and then crouched to run his hand across the terry cloth. Both damp. Had they both showered last night before going out or had Kip taken a quick shower early this morning after waking up alone?

A little bottle of motel shampoo lay on its side in the shower caddy next to a bar of soap. A toothbrush, small tube of toothpaste and spray can of deodorant were scattered on the counter next to the sink. A see-through toiletry bag hung on a hook on the back of the door.

He got up close to the door and peered into the bag. If he thought he'd find a syringe in there, the face cream, hair gel and dental floss just quashed that hope. Junkies used dental floss?

He dumped everything in the trash can and joined Nina

in the bedroom. She'd moved the suitcase to the bed and had tucked the clothes back inside.

Throwing up her hands, she said, "I didn't find anything in here out of the ordinary, but I guess the cops already knew that, which is why they let us in."

"Nothing in the bathroom. If she took the fatal overdose here in this room, there's no evidence of it now."

"Maybe Kip cleaned up when he took his stuff and left." She stood in the middle of the floor with her hands on her hips. "I guess that's everything—oops—except these jeans on the back of the chair."

She took two steps to the chair and plucked the jeans from it. She swung them through the air and a piece of paper fluttered to the carpet. She stooped to sweep it up.

"What's that?" Jase flipped back the covers of the bed in case Nina hadn't thought to do it. Nothing.

"It's a cocktail napkin from Mandy's."

"If you want to toss it on top of this pizza box, I'll take all the trash out to the Dumpster container I saw around the corner." Jase picked up the edge of the box, vowing to swear off pepperoni pizza for the next year.

"Okay." She shook out the napkin. "There's writing on it."

"Anything important?"

"I don't think so. Just one word." She tugged on each side of the white square.

"What?"

"Tempest."

Chapter Eleven

The room spun. He gripped the pizza box, crushing the cardboard. "What did you say?"

Holding up the napkin, she waved it in the air. "Tempest. You know, like the Shakespeare play, or I guess that was *The Tempest*. Or maybe it means tempest in a teapot or she's referring to the oncoming storm."

"Is it Lou's handwriting?"

"As far as I can tell." She crumpled the napkin in her fist and chucked it at the pizza box, still clutched in his hand.

He dipped to catch the balled-up napkin on top of the box, amazed at the steadiness of his hands when his mind was racing in a million different directions. "I'll take this out. Anything else need to go in the Dumpster container?"

"Was there anything in the bathroom?"

"Just used toiletries. I put them in the trash can. Housekeeping can get rid of it when they clean the room."

"Nothing else in here. I'll locate Lou's mother, Inez, and see if she wants Lou's clothes and the contents of her purse. I'm guessing Inez will come out and handle Lou's apartment in Portland."

"I'll take this stuff out while you give the room a once-over."

As Nina pulled out the drawer of the nightstand, Jase

headed for the door, holding the pizza box as if it were a silver platter and the crumpled napkin a bottle of nitro-glycerine.

The napkin with Simon's agency printed on it in Lou's pocket certainly did have an explosive quality about it. Why the hell had Lou written *Tempest* on that napkin? What did she know about Tempest? She hadn't even known Simon.

Had Chris Kitchens mentioned Tempest to Lou? His step faltered on the way to the Dumpster container. Was Chris Kitchens really Simon's brother? They'd had only his word for it.

That, and a striking resemblance.

This afternoon, he'd request a background on Kitchens that he should've requested before allowing him anywhere near Nina. He'd done that for Kip Chandler already and he'd checked out as a small-time thief and junkie from Seattle whose brother the attorney had gotten out of a few scrapes.

When he reached the Dumpster container, he smoothed out the napkin on top of the cardboard, folded it and slipped it into his pocket. Lou had heard that name from someone—and he planned to find out from whom.

By the time he returned to the motel room, Nina had zipped up Lou's bag and parked it next to the door.

"I think that's everything. The police have her purse at the station, and…and I guess I can pick up her clothes from the hospital, where they took her for the autopsy."

He wedged a finger beneath the chin she'd dropped to her chest. "Are you okay? I know you and Lou had a difficult relationship, but she was your stepsister, your father's daughter."

Her chin quivered and one tear rolled down her smooth skin. "Maybe she's at peace now. It's all I can hope for."

He caught the tear on the edge of his thumb. "I'm sorry

it was so hard, but it doesn't sound as if Lou could've had a normal relationship with anyone."

"She couldn't. Maybe she even scared away Kip."

"I don't think Kip was as out of it as he pretended to be."

"Really? Why do you say that?"

"I don't know." He yanked up the handle of Lou's suitcase and tipped it on its wheels. "Something about his eyes—too sharp to be totally wasted."

Tilting her head, she pulled open the door. "So, what was he doing with Lou?"

"Beats the hell outta me." He rolled the bag through the door. "Maybe Lou talked up the B and B to him, told him it was hers. He thought she had some money coming and tagged along to Break Island. When it became clear to him that she didn't have a shot at Moonstones and was into heavier stuff than he was, he hightailed it out of here."

"I have no clue. Lou always seemed to run with an entourage—big or small. She accused me of collecting men to take care of me, but she did the same. I guess we were both affected by playing second fiddle to our parents' great love."

"Lou must've had issues before her parents' divorce and her father's remarriage to your mom."

"I did, too."

Jase hoisted Lou's suitcase into the back of the truck and hooked his thumb in his belt loop. "Your father's abandonment?"

"It's hard growing up without a dad." She folded her hands across her belly. "And here I am about to do the same thing to my child."

"Hey." He took her by the shoulders. "Through no fault of your own. You split up with Simon before you knew you were pregnant, right?"

She nodded.

"You tried to reach him, right?"

"Maybe not hard enough."

"There's no way you were going to find him."

"What?" Her forehead furrowed.

"I mean, if he didn't want to be found, you weren't going to find him." The napkin from Lou's jeans burned a hole in his pocket. Had Simon somehow reached out to Lou before he was killed?

"Simon knew about Lou, didn't he?"

"Knew about her but had never met her. When he started…acting weird, I told him I'd witnessed firsthand what could happen when mental illness went untreated. He'd heard all the stories about Lou. Why do you ask?"

He steered her toward the passenger side of the truck. "Just that—just wondering if he knew you'd dealt with erratic behavior before."

"Oh, yeah. He knew."

As he pulled away from The Sandpiper, he made a right turn and Nina put her hand on his arm. "Where are you going?"

"I want to head down to the harbor and see if anyone gave Chris a ride back to the mainland. If not, he checked out of The Sandpiper after midnight and waited around for about five hours for the next ferry out of here, which makes no sense at all."

Nina wrinkled her nose. "You don't think Pruitt and Chief Hazlett already checked that out?"

"I think Pruitt and the chief believe Lou's death was a simple overdose. Case closed. This is a small-town department and they don't have the resources to run around checking out possible leads on a hunch."

"What are you saying, Jase? Do you think Chris had something to do with Lou's death? Why? What possible motive could Chris have had for killing a woman he'd just met?"

Tempest. Why had Lou written that word? What did Chris Kitchens know about his brother's work and eventual breakdown?

He squeezed her knee. "That thought didn't occur to you?"

Nina plowed her fingers through her hair. "I don't know what to think, Jase. As far as I know, Lou hadn't been using H for years. Of course, it doesn't mean she didn't try it again. Maybe that's why it killed her. She'd been used to a certain amount but her body couldn't handle that anymore after being clean."

"Could be. I just need to satisfy my curiosity."

And to protect Nina.

After driving through town, he swung the truck into the parking lot for the wharf, busy with fishing boats and the tourist ferry that hopped from island to island. "Where are the private boats?"

She tapped the glass. "On the far side by the bait shop."

He parked and Nina was out of the truck in a flash. Did she half hope that Lou's death wasn't an accidental overdose? Maybe she was afraid that Lou had taken her own life, just as her father had done, and felt guilty that her stepsister might have done it because of her pregnancy.

And she didn't even know about Tempest.

He trailed after her as she marched up to a man working on his powerful-looking Wellcraft boat.

Nina balanced one foot on the boat and his heart skipped a beat. Then he took a long breath of salty air. He couldn't wrap Nina in cotton. Despite all the stress swirling around her, she was taking care of herself.

She called out to the man, who still hadn't seen her. "Good morning. Can I ask you a question?"

The man looked up from his work and pushed his cap back on his head, squinting at her with his already squinty eyes. "Yes, ma'am?"

"Do you take people to the mainland?"

He took her in and then shifted his gaze to Jase. "Depends on who's asking, a potential customer or the state transportation agency."

"Oh, I'm not—" she flung her arm back at Jase "—we're not from any agency. I just want to know if you took a friend of mine to the mainland earlier this morning—like really early."

He dropped his shoulders and adjusted his cap again. "I took a couple over about two hours ago. That's it."

"Okay, thanks." She backed off the boat.

His voice stopped her. "You might check with Steve down that way. He's the one with the Hewescraft aluminum boat about three slips over. I overheard him in the coffee shop this morning complaining about an early morning fare."

"Thanks."

Jase took her arm as if to steady her on the bumpy metal of the gangplank.

"Even if Steve did take Chris over this morning, what does it prove, Jase?"

"It proves that he left the island instead of checking out of the motel and then hanging around for a few hours to wait for the ferry, which makes no sense."

"Whether he hung around or left immediately, it doesn't necessarily implicate him in or exonerate him from Lou's death."

"Once that autopsy report comes back, it could."

He slowed his steps. "Maybe we should let the cops do their job." Or Prospero. The less Nina was directly involved in the destruction Tempest left in its wake, the better. She didn't need the added stress of investigating Lou's death.

She stopped and widened her stance, just in case he thought she was about to topple over. "Jase, you're not my protector. You're supposed to be fixing my B and B, not me."

He should've investigated this on his own. His lids fell half-mast over his eyes and his mouth hardened for a split second. "You don't need to prove anything here. Lou treated you badly until the very end."

"She was my stepfather's daughter. I owe it to Bruce to figure out what happened."

Stepping back, he gestured her toward the boat. "Have at it, Nancy Drew."

She brushed past him, rolling her eyes. Controlling and high-handed, just like Simon.

The next boat owner—Steve—was working on his engine when they walked up. She had to wave to get his attention over the roar of the motor.

He cut the engine and wiped his hands on a greasy cloth he had sitting on the deck behind him. "Do you need a ride to the mainland? It's a good thing you're gettin' while the gettin's good. Once that monster storm hits, there will be no crossing this sound."

"Actually, we're not. I live on the island. Do you know Moonstones?"

"I know Bruce Moore's daughter was found there this morning—dead. OD'd just like we all expected her to one day."

"Lou Moore was my stepsister."

He scratched his grizzled jaw. "Sorry, young lady. You must be the other daughter. If it's not a ride you're after, what can I do for you?"

Jase wedged a foot against the boat. "We'd like some information about your early fare this morning."

Steve uttered a curse and spat into the water. "I didn't have a fare this morning. I got a call from a guy after midnight wanting a ride over, told him I'd meet him here, and he never showed up."

"Did you call him back?"

"I sure did. He wouldn't pick up. I thought maybe someone poached my ride, but if they did, nobody's fessing up to it."

Nina reached for her phone and cupped it in her hand. "Do you still have the number on your phone? I just want to see if it's my friend. I thought he was leaving the island last night. If he didn't, I might have to take him over today."

"Why don't you just call him?"

"I tried." She shrugged. "Same result as you. He won't pick up or his phone's dead or something. Do you mind?"

"Nope." He chuckled. "In fact, if you're an angry girlfriend, the guy deserves it."

He reached for his cell phone sitting on a deck bin and tapped the screen. "Here it is. You ready?"

She displayed Chris's number and nodded. He read off the exact number on her display, and her heart somersaulted.

"That's not his number. Thanks anyway."

He saluted and went back to work.

She pivoted and stepped off the gangplank onto the sidewalk that led to the parking lot.

"Are we done interrogating people for the day?"

She tapped her phone against her chin. "That was Chris's number."

Jase raised his brows. "Why'd you lie to Steve?"

"I didn't want to get into any long discussion with him. Why would Chris try to get off the island after checking out of the motel and then change his mind?"

"I don't know, Nina. Maybe we should just leave this alone. I need to get back to my laptop."

She covered her mouth with her hand. "Of course you do. Sorry for dragging you all over town when you have work to do."

"I was happy to do it, and I think I was the one doing the dragging."

When they got back into the truck, he started the engine and turned to her. "I have a question for you."

She formed a cross with two fingers and held them in front of her face. "Don't ask me why I'm running around, trying to figure out Lou's last hours on earth."

"I'm not. I wasn't." Stretching his arms in front of him, he clasped the steering wheel. "You know those jeans you found on the back of the chair in Lou's motel room?"

"Yeah?"

"Was she wearing those jeans when we saw her earlier in the night?"

A clothing question. She blinked. "I don't think so. No. The jeans she had on the last time I saw her had metal studs along the back pockets, and those are the jeans she had on when she died."

He pulled out of the parking lot and turned down the road toward the other side of town, toward Moonstones.

She studied his profile, which gave away nothing. "Why are you asking about Lou's jeans?"

"Just curious about the piece of paper in the pocket."

"The piece of paper?" She wrinkled her nose, trying to remember the word. Snapping her fingers, she said, "Tempest."

"That's right." He paused for two beats. "Does it mean anything to you?"

"No. Should it?"

"You never heard it before?"

"Well, yeah, I've heard the word before, but not in any context related to Lou, except that she created a tempest wherever she went."

Jase narrowed his eyes and drilled the road ahead. "Creating trouble everywhere."

"That was Lou." Her fidgeting fingers pleated the hem of her shirt. Were they even discussing Lou anymore?

He blew out a breath that turned into a whistle. "She won't be causing any trouble now."

When they returned to Moonstones, all Nina's curiosity and energy had been overtaken by a leaden lethargy.

Jase had brought Lou's suitcase into the house and Nina wheeled it into the corner, swallowing a lump in her throat.

"Are you going to write?"

"Do you need anything before I do?"

"I'm going to take a nap. Now that I've gotten over most of the nausea, the thing that bothers me most about this pregnancy is how it saps my energy in the middle of the day sometimes."

"You hardly had any sleep last night, so I wouldn't blame it on the pregnancy."

"That's true." She stopped at the corner of the staircase. "Do you need anything before I drift off to dreamland?"

"I'm good." He turned toward the guest rooms on the other side of the sitting room.

"Jase?"

He stopped and answered without turning around. "Yeah?"

"Thanks for everything…I mean last night, for holding me. I don't think I would've fallen asleep on my own."

His back stiffened but still he didn't turn around. "It was…nothing. No problem. Glad I was here to help."

He continued across the room and she didn't stop him.

It was nothing. He'd said so. He just had one of those take-charge kinds of personalities—just like Simon—and what better way to indulge it than with a pregnant woman?

Why would he be remotely attracted to a woman carrying another man's baby? Especially a man she'd admitted was half out of his mind. As if she hadn't dragged Jase

Buckley into enough crazy. If she didn't watch it, he'd change his war story into a story about a crazy family starring drugs, suicide and demented ex-fiancés.

She clicked the bedroom door shut behind her and sat on the edge of the bed to pull off her boots.

Her eyes flicked to the window. Why had Lou come here to die? Maybe she'd shot up on the deck. That would be just like her to defile the place where Mom had died and that was so special to their parents.

But if she had injected a syringe full of heroin into her veins on the deck of Moonstones, she hadn't been alone. The CSI team hadn't found any drug paraphernalia on the deck, so someone would've had to remove it.

Is that what Chris had been doing while waiting for the morning ferry? Or is that why Kip had disappeared?

She rolled over and punched her pillow. Maybe Kip and Chris and Simon were all in the same place.

And they could all stay there as far as she was concerned.

NINA AWOKE WITH a start and a pounding heart. She ran her tongue along the inside of her dry mouth, dread thudding through her veins.

The last time she'd been startled awake, her stepsister had turned up dead on the deck outside.

She sat up and scooted to the edge of the bed, her head cocked, listening for…whatever. She eased forward to peer through the drapes at the window and a glorious pink-and-orange sky greeted her. The calm before the storm.

She glanced at the clock. She'd slept away the afternoon. Hopefully, Jase had gotten some work done.

She rubbed her eyes and crossed the room. Still on alert, she pushed open her bedroom door and walked down the hallway that connected her rooms to the rest of the B and B.

She opened the door at the end of the hall and heard the clicking of a keyboard.

"Jase?"

"I'm here. Did you sleep well?"

She massaged the back of her neck and entered the sitting room, where Jase had set up shop near the window. She sauntered across the room, approaching him from behind, but if she'd hoped to catch a glimpse of his book, he disappointed her by minimizing his active window.

"Are you one of those writers who won't share his work in progress?"

"I don't know if I'm one of those writers. It's all new to me. I don't even know if it's any good." He drummed his thumbs on the edge of the keyboard. "You slept for a long time. Do you feel better?"

"Not about Lou's death, but in general I do."

"Hungry?"

She yawned. "I suppose I am, but I'm not up for cooking."

"And you don't want to taste my cooking. I can pick something up—just not pizza."

"What's the matter with pizza?" She bumped her forehead with the heel of her hand as she remembered the stale-pizza smell from Lou's motel room. "No pizza. There's a Chinese place that delivers."

"Sounds good."

"I already have the number saved to my cell phone." Still yawning, she shuffled to the front door, where she'd hung her purse on a hook, and retrieved her phone.

The display showed two text messages—one from her demanding client in LA and one from a friend asking if she was still alive.

As she responded to her friend's message, a third buzzed

through. She recognized Chris Kitchens's phone number and waved the phone at Jase. "Finally, a message from Chris."

"What's it say?"

She held the phone to her face and peered at the words as she read them aloud. "'Leave the island. Your life is in danger.'"

Chapter Twelve

Jase's heart slammed against his chest. Why would Chris be warning Nina?

She looked up from the display, her face drained of all color. "He found Simon."

"Wait. What?" He ran a hand over his face. His mind had been traveling a completely different course, but Nina had reached a logical conclusion...for her.

"He doesn't say that in the message, does he?" He thrust out his hand and she dropped the phone in his palm as if she couldn't get rid of it fast enough.

The message stated only what Nina had read aloud. "He doesn't mention Simon."

"What else could it be? Lou's dead and she never posed a grave threat to me."

"Yeah, you keep saying that."

"She doesn't pose a threat now." She pointed to the phone in his hand. "But someone does—and that some-one has to be Simon."

It couldn't be Simon, but he couldn't tell her that—not yet.

"Text him back." He held out the phone to her. "Ask him where he is, who's threatening you."

"It has to be Simon." She took the phone from him and flicked it with her finger. "That's the connection with Chris."

"Your stepsister just turned up dead and Chris was one of the last people to see her alive. Maybe this has something to do with Lou. You have no idea what Lou could've been into."

He shoved his hand into his pocket, toying with the corner of the napkin. While Nina had slept, he called Jack with this latest development. Jack had theorized that Tempest had somehow contacted Lou, even if she didn't know who and what they were.

If so, Jase's job had just gotten more serious than protecting Nina from crazy family members, and he'd have to somehow back down from his personal involvement or risk putting her in danger.

"Text him, Nina. Find out what he knows."

She sat down on the edge of a bar stool and texted with her thumbs.

She stared at her phone for almost a minute and then set it down on the counter and slid off the stool. "Done. Maybe he'll respond with some information I can actually use instead of some vague warning."

Jase massaged his temples. He didn't like any of this. First Lou and now Chris—two people seemingly unconnected to the threat that Tempest could be posing to Nina—now all somehow related.

"You're worried, aren't you?"

"Huh?" He dropped his hands. He had to stop telegraphing his emotions to her and put on his poker face. "It's a text message from a guy you barely know. Maybe he's referring to the big storm on its way. He seemed spooked by it."

She pursed her lips and tapped her toe. "You can't be serious."

"We won't know what he means until he communicates more. In the meantime, you have your shotgun and you have me." And his Glock 23 pistol.

She widened her eyes. "Do you think it'll come to that? Do you think Simon would come here and try something?"

Simon again.

"Why would Simon want to hurt you if he knows you're carrying his baby?"

She covered her stomach with both hands. "I don't know. He changed. If his own brother is warning me against…"

"Hang on." Jase sliced a hand through the air. "We don't know anything yet. Don't jump to conclusions."

Totally wrong conclusions, since a dead man didn't pose a threat to anyone—neither did a dead woman. Since both Simon and Lou could be ruled out, why did Chris believe Nina's life was in danger?

"You're right." She tucked her hair behind one ear. "I'm going to order that Chinese food. Any requests?"

"Anything is fine with me."

"Spicy?"

"The spicier, the better, but—" he made a vague circle in the air in the general direction of her midsection "—can you handle spicy?"

"Oh, yeah. I think this kid's going to be born with steam coming out of his ears with the amount of spicy food I've been putting away." She swept her phone from the counter, glanced at the display once and tapped a few buttons.

After she placed the order, she tipped her chin toward his laptop set up by the window. "Did you get much writing done this afternoon?"

"Yeah."

Writing a report and sending an encrypted email to his boss regarding Chris Kitchens definitely counted as writing.

"You can try to get in a little more before dinner arrives. I'm going to wash my face and change out of these crumpled clothes."

When he heard the click of the door to the back rooms, Jase made a beeline to Nina's cell phone, which she'd left on the kitchen counter.

He scrolled through the text messages until he saw Chris's ominous words. He committed the phone number to memory and then returned to his laptop, where he brought up his email. Then he sent a request to Prospero's tech unit to track the phone and tagged it as urgent.

While he was at it, he created a document file on his desktop and called it *Book*. What else? He typed in a chapter heading and added a few lines—not that he didn't trust Nina, but natural curiosity might lead her to snoop around his laptop—just in case she got past his password. At least she'd see a file on his desktop and he had something to work on if she kept insisting that he write.

He kept the laptop powered on in case someone at Prospero got back to him regarding Chris's cell. Then he retrieved a beer from the fridge.

"Can you please get me a glass of sparkling water? I'll set the table."

Nina had appeared looking fresh-faced and casual in a pair of black yoga pants and a soft, rose-colored T-shirt that gently hugged the swell of her belly. Her beauty made his heart skip a beat...or two.

He set down his bottle of beer before it slipped from his hand. "You mean we're not just eating out of the cartons?"

"This is *not* the edge of civilization despite your belief to the contrary."

"I'm not accusing Washingtonians of being barbarians. I like eating Chinese out of the carton."

She looked up from arranging place mats on the table, her head cocked. "I never would've had you pegged as that type."

"The type to eat out of a carton?" He laughed. "Is that a type? I thought everyone did that."

"You know, the cold-pizza-and-beer-in-the-morning type. The brush-your-teeth-with-your-finger type."

"Whoa!" He filled a glass with ice and poured flavored sparkling water over the cubes. "Let's not get crazy. I always use a toothbrush, but I've had a few cold-pizza breakfasts in my day. Did you think I ate pizza on fine china with silverware?"

She folded a napkin and placed it on one side of the place mat. "You seem cultured to me, not quite comfortable in your flannel shirts and work boots."

He stomped his feet. "I'm okay in my work boots, and I detest the ballet."

"You're from Connecticut, aren't you? Prep school. Ivy League. Lacrosse."

He took a gulp of beer. She had him pegged. "I never played lacrosse."

"A guy like you, marines, you must've gone in as an officer."

"I did. Intelligence."

"And you went to an Ivy League school?"

"Yale." Might as well tell the truth where he could.

She snapped her fingers. "Utensils, please."

He yanked open a drawer and collected a couple of forks and knives. "Did you order soup, too?"

"Hot-and-sour." She reached across the peninsula for the utensils. "You must have some good stories for your book."

"Yep."

The doorbell saved him from any other personal revelations. "I'll get it."

He approached the front door from the side and leaned to the right to peek through the peephole. A young, pimply dude shifted from side to side on the porch.

"We have delivery." He swung open the door and took the food from the delivery guy while digging in his pocket for cash.

He turned and almost bumped into Nina.

"You didn't have to pay for that. I'll get half."

"I haven't done enough work around here to earn my keep. Let me get dinner."

They popped open the cartons and shoveled the steaming food onto their plates. One spoonful of the soup cleared his sinuses.

"That baby of yours is in for a treat."

"He should have an international palate the way I've been eating."

"Have you picked out any names yet?"

"I've been thinking about William, Will for short. Do you think everyone will call him Bill or Billy?"

"Not if he calls himself Will. I trained everyone to call me Jase."

As soon as the words left his lips, he stuffed his mouth with food, hoping Nina would let them slide. No such luck.

"Your name's not Jase? It's short for Jason?"

"Yeah." He waved his fork in the air. "Too many of those where I grew up."

Would she now try to find Jason Buckley on the internet? It still wouldn't lead her to Jason or Jase Bennett. The lives of Prospero agents were not for public consumption in search engines.

What had she discovered about Simon Skinner? Since both agencies were black ops under the umbrella of the CIA, he had to believe Tempest agents had the same protections, maybe more. Prospero hadn't been able to uncover anything about Max Duvall when he'd contacted them—not until they'd requested his records from the CIA.

"Jase suits you better than Jason."

For the rest of their dinner, he turned the talk away

from his background and his real name to the baby. Nina had her worries about raising this baby on her own, but her excitement and joy about the pregnancy bubbled over despite everything.

Her happiness flowed into him and filled that hole left by Maggie and her selfishness. He ignored the red flags and soaked in the joy emanating from Nina.

As they cleaned up, Nina got a phone call from Lou's mother. She took the call in the back rooms, and Jase flipped open his laptop to check his mail.

The techies hadn't let him down. He clicked on the email and scanned the contents. The department had been able to triangulate the location of Chris's phone—he was still on the island.

What the hell was this guy's game? Had he somehow made contact with his brother, Simon, before Simon's death? Maybe Simon had sent Chris on a quest to track down Nina. Maybe the whole aw-shucks-I-just-wanna-find-my-brother shtick was an act. Was Chris here on Simon's orders? For what purpose?

Jack hadn't gotten back to him yet with a full dossier on Chris Kitchens. He should've never let the guy get anywhere near Nina without it. She didn't owe Kitchens anything.

"Whew, I'm glad that's over with." Nina walked into the room, pressing a hand to her heart. "Inez took Lou's death pretty hard."

"You didn't expect her to?" He closed out of his email.

"It's hard to tell with Inez. She's going to take care of Lou's apartment in Portland, and I'm going to ship Lou's things to her there."

"And the funeral?"

"Once the coroner gets the toxicology report and releases the body, I'm going to send her to Portland—to her mother." She swiped a tear from her cheek. "Lou was never happy on this island once her father married my mother."

"It doesn't sound like Lou was ever happy."

"Some people are like that."

"But not you."

"I try." She rubbed her nose. "Why do you say that?"

"You have a lot going on right now and you still have a great attitude, a great attitude about your pregnancy."

"I always wanted children and I thought Simon was the one, but life doesn't always turn out the way you plan it."

"That's for sure." He reached across the table and picked up his bottle and her glass. "Do you want more sparkling water? A cup of tea?"

"More water, please. That food made me thirsty. Are you having another beer?"

"No." He cocked his head. "Is that your phone buzzing? Mine's not set to buzz."

She dived for her phone charging on the kitchen counter and touched the display. "It's another message from Chris."

"Does he give any more details about this threat?"

She looked up from the phone, her tongue darting from her mouth. "He wants to meet me. He must still be on the island."

He put on his surprised look—raised eyebrows and open mouth. "I'll be damned. What does he say?"

She held the phone in front of her. "Meet me at the wharf in town at ten o'clock. I'll tell you what I know. Then get me off this island."

"Why can't he tell you in his text or, better yet, call you?"

"It sounds like he needs a way off Break Island and wants to make sure I provide that way."

"I don't like it, Nina. Tell him I'll go in your place."

"Jase…"

"Tell him." He jabbed a finger in the air. "You're not putting yourself or your baby in jeopardy for this guy."

She texted Chris back and held the phone cupped in her hand, waiting for a response.

Jase's muscles tensed, his breath short.

Nina's phone buzzed and she shook her head. "He said he doesn't trust you. He doesn't trust anyone. It has to be me."

"I'm coming with you, and don't even ask him if that's okay."

Her thumbs danced across her phone's screen, and again she waited for the answering buzz. Even so, she jumped when it sounded off. She blew out a breath.

"He wants us to take a boat to the town harbor. He'll tell me what's going on when we're on the way to the mainland."

"We still have the arrangement with the Kleinschmidts. We can use their boat."

She glanced at her display again. "We have just over an hour."

He traced a line down the side of her arm. "Are you sure you want to do this? He can find his own way back to the mainland."

"I have to know. I have to know if Simon is out there and what he wants from me." She held the phone to her chest with both hands. "I told you, I sensed he was stalking me in LA. I just want to find out what he hopes to gain by this behavior."

Spreading his hands, he said, "It might not be about Simon at all. It might have something to do with Lou. Maybe you were right about her death—maybe Kip Chandler had something to do with it."

"That's just it, Jase. They all headed back to the same motel together, so Chris may have heard something, or seen something with Lou and Kip, that I need to know.

Something that may not mean a lot to the police, but would mean a heck of a lot to me." She placed her hand over his, still on her arm. "I have to meet Chris to find out."

Her skin against his felt soft and warm but electrifying. Did she feel it, too? He looked into her blue eyes and caught an answering spark.

Jerking his head to the side, he broke the connection. This was wrong on so many levels he couldn't even begin to count them. "We'll come prepared."

She paused for two beats, and when she responded, her voice had a hoarse edge. "I can't exactly bring my shotgun."

She felt it, too, this thing between them, and she didn't even know who he was. It was all a lie.

He turned from her and grabbed his backpack, which was hanging over the back of the chair at the desk. He reached for his weapon. "I don't want to freak you out, but I'm bringing this."

When he faced her holding his Glock pistol, barrel down, her eyebrows shot up.

"Why do you have that?"

"I'm a former marine. I have a conceal-and-carry permit. It's all legal."

"None of that answers the question I asked."

He parked the gun next to his laptop. "Sure it does. I'm an ex-marine. Carrying is second nature to me."

"Okay, so you'll be the one with the gun this time. Just don't shoot anybody." She formed her fingers into a gun and pulled the trigger. "I'm going to change into something warmer."

Jase snagged his own jacket from the hook by the front door and shoved his weapon into the pocket. He'd leave the pocket zipped—until they got to the town wharf. He didn't know what to expect from Chris Kitchens, but he wasn't going to take any chances—not with Nina's life and not with Will's.

His child had been a boy, too, until Maggie carelessly ended his life. He hadn't even gotten used to the idea of being a father before it was all over in the blink of an eye. He hadn't been able to protect his son, but he sure as hell could protect Nina's.

She came from the back wearing jeans, a bulky green sweater and deck shoes. She pointed to his jacket. "Do you want something waterproof? The water's getting choppy out there and it still might rain."

He glanced down at his down jacket in his hands. "This isn't waterproof?"

"That may be waterproof for Connecticut rain, but not for a storm on the water in the sound." She flung open the door of the closet in the foyer and pulled out a black full-length slicker. "Bruce wasn't as tall as you, but this will cover most of what needs to be covered."

He pulled on the coat, which hung just past his knees and rode up his wrists, but it was roomy enough. "This'll do."

"Let's go see about that boat."

"I'll go see about the boat. You wait here. Have some hot tea."

"Anyone ever tell you that you are bossy, Buckley?"

"All the time."

He prepped the boat for departure and returned to find Nina rinsing out a cup in the sink.

"I took your advice and had some tea. Now I'm unstoppable."

"You're not unstoppable, so don't even think about doing anything dumb."

She wedged a hand on her hip. "What exactly do you think I'm going to do, take Chris down?"

"I hope it doesn't come to that."

"Do you think it would be better if I showed up alone?"

"Absolutely not. Didn't we already discuss this? I'm not going to allow you to put yourself in danger. I'm not going to allow you to put Will in danger."

By the way Nina's mouth hung open, he realized he'd stepped over the line—way over the line.

"Hold on there, Papa Bear. I didn't mean I'd actually show up by myself. You'd be there, just hidden away."

The heat clawed up his chest, disguised by the double layer of clothing he'd piled on.

"Sorry I overreacted. Maybe it's my imagination working overtime, but I don't trust Chris Kitchens as far as I can drop-kick him." If Jack would get back to him on Kitchens's background, he might be going into this meeting a little less twitchy.

She tilted her head, and her ponytail swung over her shoulder. "I appreciate your concern, but I'm not going to do anything to harm my baby. In fact, I'm doing this to protect him. If Chris has information about some threat to me, I want to know about it."

"Fair enough." He pulled his weapon from his down jacket and held it up. "And if Chris Kitchens is the actual threat, I'll know about that soon enough."

"Okay, then. Is the boat ready to go?"

"All set."

She locked up Moonstones, and they crossed the dark yard to the Kleinschmidts' boat.

He gunned the motor and flicked on the spotlights, which illuminated the lapping water. The trip to the town wharf couldn't be more than ten minutes, but judging from the choppy water, it would be a rough ten minutes.

"Do you get seasick?"

"No, do you? This ain't like sailing on some calm bay, preppy boy."

He laughed, and the wind snatched the sound and

rolled it over the waves. "Okay, pioneer girl of the Pacific Northwest. Did you fly up from LA or come over in a covered wagon?"

She punched him in the side, which he barely felt.

The boat chugged into the water, which slapped its sides, sending salty spray into the air. The mist clung to his eyelashes and moistened his lips, where he licked it off.

The ten-minute trip turned into fifteen as he negotiated the waves, riding them up and down. As the lights from the wharf grew brighter, he reduced his speed and shouted, "Is it very busy this time of night?"

"No, but I expect it to be busier than usual as people try to make their way off the island before the storm hits."

"Why do you suppose Chris isn't among them? Why does he need a ride from you?"

"I don't know. Maybe he figures out on the water is the safest place to warn me."

He aimed the boat toward an empty slip and crawled into the harbor. Streetlamps every fifty feet or so cast a glow on the boats bobbing in their slips.

"Chris better be keeping an eye out for us, because I'm not going to let you wander around looking for him and I sure as hell am not going to, either."

"He's the one who set this up."

He pulled into the slip, and as the boat bumped the boat dock bumpers, he tossed a rope to Nina. "Are we supposed to pay for the slip?"

"Not if we're doing a quick in-and-out."

"I guess that depends on Chris."

Jase left on the boat's lights to create a circle of illumination on the wooden walkway fronting the boats. He didn't want any surprises from Kitchens.

A boat started several slips over and they both turned to look.

"Where is this guy?"

"Are you jumpy or what?" Nina sat on the storage bin. "We just got here."

Jase felt for the gun in the pocket of the mackinaw. Definitely jumpy. "I thought he was in a big hurry to leave the island. Maybe he got a ride on Kip's helicopter."

Nina snorted. Then she put down the boat's stepladder and climbed over. Glancing one way and then the other, she called out softly, "Chris?"

Jase vaulted over the side of the boat to join her, his feet landing with a clang on the gangplank that echoed in the night. He shoved his hand into his pocket and gripped his gun.

Something didn't smell right, and he didn't mean the fishy odor that permeated the air. Had that even been Kitchens texting Nina? Anyone with access to his phone could be sending her messages.

Someone halfway down the line of boats shouted.

Nina's head jerked up. "What was that?"

"Someone yelling down there."

The voice rose again and a few boats turned on their spotlights.

"What do you think is going on?"

"I have no idea." But he had an uneasy feeling in his gut.

A man burst out of the bait shop and started running toward the lights.

Nina took two steps toward the commotion. "Jase."

Something about the men's shouts chilled his blood. Nina must've heard it, too.

She took two more steps.

"Wait, Nina."

"I heard… I heard…" Her shoes pounded against the damp wood as she ran toward the agitated knot of people at the water's edge.

He had no choice but to follow her, his weapon banging

against his thigh. He reached her before she reached the clutch of people, all talking and pointing at once.

They approached the group together and Jase asked, "What's going on?"

The boater they'd talked to earlier that day pointed at the brackish water lapping against the side of his boat. "It looks like...I don't know, something."

Jase grabbed the flashlight from him and crouched on the silver gangplank, leaning forward as the beam of light played over the water.

Something floated out from beneath the gangplank and everyone behind him gasped and jumped back.

It was something all right—it was Chris Kitchens's dead body.

Chapter Thirteen

Nina stumbled against Jase, almost falling over him. "It's Chris."

"You know this guy?" The man from the bait shop squatted next to Jase.

The boater snapped his fingers. "Is that the one you were asking about this morning? The ex-boyfriend?"

Three pairs of eyes drilled into her. She put her hands over her face. This was getting crazy and she couldn't even keep her own lies straight.

"Yes. No. I didn't say he was my boyfriend."

Jase refocused the flashlight on the group. "We do know this man, however. Has someone called 9-1-1 yet?"

Thank God for Jase taking charge. She was finding it hard to even stand up.

Steve, the boater from earlier in the day, scratched his chin. "Hell, I didn't even know if it was really a body or not. I thought I saw a face in the water. Scared the hell out of me."

The bait shop owner held up his phone. "I got it."

While he made the call, Nina tried to catch Jase's eye, but he was busy trying to haul in the body—Chris.

"I think he's stuck on something beneath the slip."

"Maybe we should just let the professionals handle this."

"Bubbles!" Jase flattened out on his belly and scooted closer to Chris's floating head. "I saw bubbles. He's not dead."

Jase shed her stepfather's coat and slid into the black water as Nina screamed his name.

"I'll be damned." The boater dropped to his knees and aimed the flashlight where Jase had disappeared.

Nina released a breath when Jase popped up again, keeping Chris's head above the surface.

Jase coughed and shook wet hair from his eyes. "His leg is pinned. Hold him up while I release him."

Steve leaned forward and hooked his arms beneath Chris's armpits while Jase dived down again.

Nina wrapped her arms around her body to stop the shivering, but it wasn't the cold that was causing it.

Sirens wailed and the emergency vehicles lit up the pier.

Finally, Jase rose from the murky depths and the rest of Chris's body floated to the surface.

The EMTs did the rest as they hauled Chris from the water. They pumped his chest.

"Is he alive?" She hovered on the outside of the circle of EMTs working on Chris.

A cop stepped in front of her. "Ma'am, you're going to have to give them room."

She spun around and grabbed Jase, soaking wet and freezing cold to the touch. "What were you thinking, jumping in that water?"

"He was alive, Nina. I saw bubbles at the surface of the water."

"That could've been anything."

"She has a point there. There're all kinds of things bubbling in that water." The bait shop owner shook his head. "He sure looked like a goner to me."

A police officer approached them with a pad of paper in one hand. "I'm Officer Franklin. Who discovered him?"

Steve raised his hand. "That's my boat. I was going to ready her for a trip to the mainland when I saw something white floating beside her."

"He yelled out and I'm parked right next door." The other boat owner thrust his thumb over his shoulder. "I came over to see what all the commotion was about. I saw Ned step out of his shop and called him over, and then these two showed up."

The cop wagged his finger between her and Jase. "And what were you two doing out here?"

Jase poked her in the small of her back. "Nina's step-sister died earlier this morning. I was just taking her back to this side of the island because she left something in her sister's motel room."

"Oh, yeah." Franklin tapped his chin with the eraser of his pencil. "Louise Moore. Sorry for your loss, ma'am, but couldn't you two just walk from the dune side of the island?"

"We had the boat out anyway."

Nina nodded, marveling at the easy lies that sprang to Jase's lips. She supposed it was best the cops didn't know they'd come here to meet Chris, but wouldn't they discover that anyway once they checked out his cell phone and saw his texts to her number?

The EMTs pulled a white sheet over Chris's face, and Nina swayed. Jase caught her around the waist.

"Is he gone?"

The EMTs strapped Chris's body to the gurney. "He's gone."

The cop circled his pencil in the air. "Does anyone know who he is?"

Would Jase lie about this, too?

He cleared his throat. "His name is Chris Kitchens.

He's related to a friend of Ms. Moore's. We met him for the first time yesterday and figured he'd left the island today."

Steve shoved a toothpick between his lips. "This isn't the boyfriend?"

"Boyfriend?" Nina ran her tongue along her bottom lip. "I think you misunderstood. He's related to an ex-boyfriend."

"Does anyone know next of kin?"

Ned was already heading for his bait shop and Steve shrugged his shoulders. "Don't know a thing about him."

"Like I said, we just met him yesterday. He was looking for his brother, whom he hadn't seen since they were both adopted over twenty years ago." Jase draped the mackinaw over his shoulders. "We couldn't help him."

"Anyone plan on leaving the island anytime soon?"

Nina rubbed her eyes as the EMTs began loading Chris's body into the back of the ambulance. "I live here now, not going anywhere."

"Just in case." Franklin put away his notepad. "We'll see what the autopsy turns up. Could be he took a wrong turn, fell into the water, hit his head and drowned."

Nina doubted that scenario, but unless she wanted to spend the rest of the night at the police station, she'd keep her mouth shut.

"If it's okay, I'm going to get him home before icicles start forming on the end of his nose." She took Jase's arm and pulled him toward the parking lot.

He resisted. "The boat."

"You're not going back on the water. We'll get a taxi back and fetch the boat tomorrow morning."

Officer Franklin spoke up. "I'll give you two a ride back. Moonstones, right?"

"That's it." Everyone here already knew her business. She wouldn't be surprised if the officer knew about Chris's contact with her stepsister before she OD'd. "Did you find Chris's phone?"

"Just his wallet, no phone. Maybe it fell in the water."

Even more reason to keep quiet about her connection to Chris, since the police department wouldn't discover anything without that phone.

Jase's teeth chattered on and off during the ride back to the B and B, so she threaded her fingers through his and squeezed his hand every time a chill claimed his body.

He leaned forward and spoke through the mesh separating the front seat from the back. "Sorry I'm getting water all over your backseat."

"That's okay. It's seen a lot worse."

Franklin wheeled his patrol car in front of Moonstones. "Are you two going to be okay?"

"As soon as I dry off and warm up, I'll be fine. Damn, I could've sworn he still had breath in him."

"Tough break. We'll be in touch."

They scrambled from the car and Nina ran ahead of Jase to open the front door. "Why is it every time we come back here, one of us is all wet?"

"It's an island."

She shoved him from behind. "Go get some warm, dry clothes on and I'll get the fire started—then we talk."

He planted his feet on the floor. "Sit down and relax. I'll start the fire when I come back. In the meantime, crank on the furnace. I'm going to hop in the shower for a few minutes first."

She didn't argue with him, since he'd somehow come to the conclusion that pregnancy sapped a woman's strength and energy—and reason, come to think of it.

She sat meekly on the edge of the chair, and as soon as she heard his door shut, she crouched before the fireplace and lit the kindling. Jase had already stacked the logs in the grate.

Fanning the fire to life, she stared into the depths of the flames. What had just happened? Chris had been the one to warn her and he'd wound up dead. No way was that a coincidence.

Would Simon kill his own brother? What did Chris mean to Simon anyway? They'd grown up apart. They were strangers despite Chris's romanticized vision of finding his little brother.

She'd listen to Jase's conclusions before jumping to any of her own. He seemed to discount Simon's involvement so quickly. Maybe he just couldn't imagine a man wanting to harm his own child. Jase seemed quite taken with hers.

She rubbed her belly and then ducked behind the bar to nab her stepfather's good cognac. Tea wouldn't cut it for Jase. She filled the bottom of a bowl-shaped snifter with the golden liquid and brought it to the table by the fire. Her gaze shifted to Jase's laptop.

For a writer, he sure didn't do much writing. Of course, he was living out a real-life drama with her and her problems. Maybe he was putting all this in his book.

She ran her fingers along the seamed closure of the laptop and snatched her hand back when she heard Jase emerge from his room.

"That hot shower felt good." He sauntered into the room, dark gray sweats covering his long legs and a white T-shirt hugging the muscles she'd always suspected of hiding beneath his bulky flannels.

He caught her stare. "I'm sorry. Were you expecting a smoking jacket or silk pajamas?"

She lifted the glass of cognac. "Would've gone nicely with this cognac."

"How'd you know I'd enjoy a glass of the good stuff?"

She swirled the liquid in the glass before handing it to him. "Just a guess."

He took the snifter from her, brushing her fingers in

the process, before sinking into the love seat. "I see you got the fire going anyway."

"It wasn't hard or taxing, believe it or not."

He stretched out his long legs. "Feels good."

"Don't ignore the elephant in the room." She dropped to the floor in front of his chair and hugged her knees to her chest, or at least as close as she could get them to her chest. "What happened to Chris?"

"He drowned." Jase took a sip of the cognac and watched her over the rim of the snifter.

"Someone killed him before he could warn me."

Jase's eyes flickered but he didn't jump into a denial—which scared the hell out of her.

"When I pulled him out of the water, it looked like he had an abrasion on the side of his head, but that could've happened when he fell into the water."

"Who falls off a gangplank into the water?"

"It was dark out there. Steve's boat's in the shadows."

"Just who are you trying to convince?" She rested her chin on her knees. "It's Simon."

"You think he'd kill his own brother?"

She clicked her tongue. "He didn't know Chris. He never mentioned having a brother to me once. He never discussed his birth family. As far as Simon was concerned, the people who adopted him were his parents and he had no siblings."

The amber liquid in Jase's glass sloshed from side to side as another chill rolled through his body.

"Scoot over." She hopped to her feet. "You're still not completely warmed up. You're going to catch a chill."

He shifted to the side of the love seat and patted the other cushion. "Be my guest."

She settled beside him and her body flushed with warmth as she remembered falling asleep in his arms the other night.

Maybe tonight he'd fall asleep in her arms.

He cupped his glass with two hands. "Have you ever reported Simon? Gotten a restraining order against him?"

"How can you get a restraining order against a ghost?"

His body stiffened. "What does that mean?"

He really was still chilled to the bone. She pressed her hands against his shoulders, pushing him forward. Then she began kneading the tight muscles between his shoulder blades with her knuckles.

"What I mean is I've never seen Simon. I haven't seen him since the day he walked out of our place." She skimmed her hands down his back, feeling the smooth flesh beneath his thin T-shirt. "I've sensed his presence or at least a presence, but you can't get a restraining order against a presence."

His muscles bunched into even tighter knots beneath her fingers.

"You're going to be sore tomorrow morning if you don't relax your muscles. You must still be chilled." She tapped his glass with her fingernail. "Drink up and have another."

He tossed back the drink and set the glass on the table with a clink. "If there is someone out there stalking you, I don't want to be drunk when he comes to your door."

She tucked her feet beneath her body and leaned against Jase's arm. "I'd put my money on you drunk or sober, Jase Buckley."

He sucked in a breath as if about to make an announcement but kissed her mouth instead.

The nutty taste of the cognac on his lips was almost enough to make *her* drunk. She melted against him, her soft breasts pressing against his rock-hard biceps.

He scooped a hand through his damp hair. "I'm sorry. I shouldn't have done that."

"Why not?" She rubbed her cheek against his shoulder.

"I've been wanting you to kiss me for the longest time. Is that… I mean, do you?" She huffed out a breath. "I'm carrying another man's baby."

He stroked her back. "And that man is gone…a ghost."

"The pregnancy was a mistake."

"Shh." He pressed two fingers against her lips. "Don't ever say that."

"I don't mean I'm upset about it or don't want my baby. I do—with all my heart. I just wanted to explain to you how it happened."

The corner of his mouth quirked into a lopsided grin. "I understand the basics."

"I mean—" she dug her fingernails into his upper arm "—how it happened with Simon, since we were having problems. The night the baby was conceived was a last-ditch effort on my part, one last attempt to reach Simon and bring him back to me."

"It didn't work."

"Sadly, no." Her bottom lip quivered. "But I have Will, and I'm glad I do. I'll never allow him to feel anything but loved and wanted, because he is."

"I believe that." He traced her lips with the tip of his finger. "I can tell you'll be a great mom."

"But first I need to keep Will safe, even if that means protecting him from his father."

"Are you going to leave the island?"

"I came here to get away, as a sanctuary, but Simon knew about Moonstones. Maybe I need to escape to a place where Simon can't reach me."

"I might be able to help you with that."

A thrill raced along her spine. Was he saying he wanted to continue their relationship?

A knock on the door made the thrill turn into a chill and she instinctively grabbed Jase's hand.

He squeezed her fingers. "Stay put."

He pushed out of the chair and stalked up to the front door. He placed his eye to the peephole. "It's Officer Franklin."

"Do you think they discovered anything yet?" She rose from the chair.

"Too soon." He opened the door. "Officer Franklin. Can we help you with anything else?"

"No, but I can help Ms. Moore."

Nina peered over Jase's shoulder. "How?"

The officer reached into his pocket and pulled out her cell phone. "You left this in the backseat of my squad car. I figured it was yours instead of Mr. Buckley's because of the pink polka-dotted case, but correct me if I'm wrong."

She held out her hand, wiggling her fingers. "It's mine. Thanks."

"No problem."

Jase asked, "Any word on Chris Kitchens?"

"Not yet. We'll keep you posted."

"Good night and thanks." Nina held up her phone. She meandered back to the love seat, hoping she and Jase could take up where they'd left off, since he'd just hinted at some kind of future for them. Her phone beeped at her.

"What was that?"

"My cell phone telling me I need to charge it." Changing course, she walked toward the kitchen to plug in the phone. She slid her finger across the display to unlock it and her pulse ticked up. "I have another text message from Chris."

Jase materialized by her side. "What does it say?"

She tapped her phone and read the message. "'I'm here. Meet—'" she shrugged "—and then gibberish."

"Gibberish?"

"Some letters and numbers."

"That's weird. Let me see it."

She handed the cell to him. "He must've sent that right

before he fell into the water or whatever happened. Look at the time."

Jase had the phone practically to his nose, and the knuckles of the hand clutching the phone were white.

Her heart skittered in her chest. "Jase, what is it?"

"The gibberish?" He turned the phone toward her. "He was typing *Tempest*."

Chapter Fourteen

"Tempest?" Nina's face registered complete and utter confusion, and then she snapped and pointed her finger at the same time. "The piece of paper in Lou's pocket. That had *tempest* written on it, too."

"That's right." The dread was pounding through his veins so relentlessly he could barely hear his own voice. He held out the phone and tapped the message. "Look, it's a *T*, 3, *N*, *P*, 3, *S*, *T*. He was definitely trying to type *Tempest*—in a hurry."

"What the hell is that all about? What does *tempest* mean? Have people started running around calling big storms tempests all of a sudden?"

"I..." He held out his hands and then clasped them together. "I'm not sure, but for both Lou and Chris to refer to Tempest and then both wind up dead, whatever it is it's not good."

"And what does it have to do with me? Do you think that's why Kip disappeared? Did we all unwittingly run across something that put us in danger?"

She was definitely on the right track. But what had Lou and Chris discovered about Tempest that Nina hadn't? The name still meant nothing to her. If the agents of Tempest were going after her to keep her quiet, they were wasting their resources. Why expend this much effort going after a dead agent's ex-fiancée to the point of killing people in the way?

It didn't make any sense.

He'd been on the verge of telling her everything, but without getting clearance from Coburn he'd be breaking all kinds of rules and maybe putting other lives in danger.

He was here to protect Nina, and that's exactly what he planned to do—whether or not she knew the reason.

"I think we need to find Kip."

"Unlike Chris, he's probably left the island by now. After hearing about Lou and Chris, I doubt Kip's going to want to be found. Who knows? Maybe his brother really does have a helicopter. He didn't strike me as the type to stick around and warn others."

"Not like Chris." She threw back her ponytail and marched to the closed door of her office.

"What are you going to do?"

"I'm going to do an internet search on *tempest*. Maybe it has some meaning we're not aware of. Maybe it's a new synthetic drug or something."

He slipped past her and stood in front of the office door, and not because he was afraid she'd find out something about the covert agency Tempest. She never would.

"It's late. You need to get some sleep. Will's had enough excitement for one day."

She reached out, her fingertips skimming the white cotton covering his chest. "Thanks for worrying about us. I'm sure you never bargained for any of this when you came to this quiet island to work."

He hadn't—not Tempest's interest in her and certainly not his own interest in her.

Tapping his head, he said, "It's all fodder for the book."

"Am I going to turn up as some crazy pregnant lady in your book?"

"You'll be the intrepid heroine." He stroked her cheek

with the back of his hand, getting lost in the blue depths of her eyes.

"Jase." She caught his hand. "Can you come into my room and talk to me while I fall asleep? I'm not sure—I just don't want to be alone right now."

"Absolutely." He brought her hand to his lips and pressed a kiss against her palm. "Get ready for bed and I'll close up shop here."

"Thanks." She spun around and headed for the back rooms.

He needed to check for any messages from Jack. He didn't have any confidential information on this computer, but he could still send messages to and receive messages from Jack. Standing over his laptop on the desk by the window, he entered his password to unlock it and then jumped as he felt a warm breath on the back of his neck.

"Sorry." Nina put a steadying hand on his arm. "I just came out to tell you not to bother with the dishes. I'll load them in the dishwasher tomorrow morning."

"Got it."

As she floated to the back of the house on her silent, stocking feet, he checked his email and then powered down the computer.

He rinsed his glass, checked the locks, turned off the lights and retrieved his Glock pistol from the mackinaw and shoved it into the pocket of his baggy sweatpants.

If he was watching over Nina tonight, he'd do so locked and loaded.

By the time he reached her room, she had changed into a pair of flannel pajamas with pink bunnies scattered across a field of white, puffy clouds.

If he'd expected her to get her sexy on, she'd just dashed those hopes.

She fluffed up a pillow against her headboard. "I'm pretty tired, but I appreciate the company."

He sat on the foot of her bed. "Are you cold? Get under the covers."

She plucked at her pajamas. "With these on? These pajamas are like wearing a blanket."

She lay on top of the bedspread and pulled a pillow beneath her head. Patting the bed, she said, "You can join me. I don't bite."

"That's a relief." But it wasn't the biting he was worried about. He was worried about the way she smelled like a field of wildflowers after a spring shower. He was worried about the way her dark hair cascaded down her back like a silky waterfall. He was worried about taking this woman, pregnant with another man's child, and claiming her as his own.

Pushing it all aside, he stretched out on the bed behind her. He slipped his weapon under the bed and rolled onto his back, staring at the ceiling.

She emitted a soft sigh as she curled an arm beneath the pillow. "Are you close with your family? Your parents? Your sister?"

She remembered he had a sister? He decided to tell the truth for once. "Not particularly. My parents didn't approve of my enlistment and I didn't approve of their disapproval."

"What did they want for you? Family business?"

Nina didn't miss a thing. How'd Simon manage to keep her in the dark for so long? "Yeah, something like that."

Of course, she didn't have to know that his family's business was politics and that she'd probably seen his father bloviating on national TV a time or two.

"Jase?"

"Yeah?" Here it came, more questions and more lies.

"Why *are* you so protective of me…and Will? Most guys would be doing an about-face if they had to deal with a pregnant woman."

He didn't have to lie about this, did he? He owed her some truthfulness.

"I was in a similar situation to yours a few years ago. My girlfriend and I had been discussing marriage, but things didn't work out."

"You broke up?"

"Yeah, and like you, Maggie found out she was pregnant after the breakup."

She rolled onto her back, her head falling to the side to study his profile. "B-but you told me you didn't have children."

"I don't." The pain that sliced through his gut surprised him. "Maggie lost the baby in her fourth month—just about where you are now."

She sucked in a quick breath. "I'm so sorry."

"It was her fault."

"Sometimes these things happen." She traced one of the bunnies with her fingertip. "I thank God every day that my pregnancy is progressing without any issues."

"At least you're not out there rock climbing."

"Rock climbing? Maggie was rock climbing going into her second trimester?"

His jaw tightened and he tried to keep the bitterness from his tone. "Can you believe that? She fell, broke her arm and lost the baby—our baby. Do you wanna know the kicker?"

She took his hand and whispered, "What?"

"I never even knew she was pregnant. She didn't tell me. I heard about the accident when I came back from an…from a trip."

"That's so unfair." She laced her fingers through his. "Is that why you jumped on me about whether or not I told Simon?"

"I guess so."

"And that's why you care so much about Will."

"It's not just Will I care about, Nina." He shifted to his side and wound a lock of her hair around his finger.

As she met his eyes, she parted her lips and he kissed her. The minty taste of her toothpaste was as sweet as honey.

"Jase, I don't know where this can go."

"Let's not worry about that right now." He touched her bottom lip with the pad of his thumb. "Go to sleep."

She turned on her right side and he pulled her lush body against his. His arm curved around her waist and his hand naturally cupped the swell of her belly.

If Tempest wanted to come after Nina, they could try but they'd have to go through him first.

NINA AWOKE ALONE in the bed. All night she'd been aware of Jase's comforting presence next to her. She'd nestled against him and felt his arms tighten around her in response.

His story about losing the baby he never knew existed had tugged at her heartstrings. It explained so much about his attitude toward her. In protecting her and Will, he hoped to make up for his missed chances with his own unborn child.

Was that the basis of his attraction, too? Once she had her baby, would Jase find another pregnant woman to nurture? It sounded crazy, but the pull of filling emotional voids in your life was strong.

She should know. Having never had a protective father figure in her life, she'd always been attracted to take-charge guys. She and Jase were a match made in psychological, subconscious heaven.

Sighing, she pushed back the covers. Jase had tucked her into bed later, but he never joined her beneath the sheets. Was he afraid of igniting the flame that kindled between them?

She was the one who had stopped the kiss last night. She wanted to know him better, find out what really made him tick. She wanted to read his book.

She tumbled out of bed and crept into the B and B's living area. Jase had flung open the drapes at the front window, allowing the gray, misty light to filter into the room.

Her breath fogged the glass as she leaned in close. She wiped a streak through it with her fist and peered outside.

It had rained again last night, harder than ever. The storm was still toying with them. Maybe it would bypass Break Island altogether.

Dressed in his Pacific Northwest uniform, Jase was leaning against a fence post he'd repaired and talking on his phone.

She didn't see him make many phone calls. His family must still be holding a grudge for his shunning of the family business, which he'd never gotten around to explaining to her. It was probably plastics or something equally staid and boring. Jase wouldn't do staid and boring—hence his stint as a marine.

He thrust his arm out to the side and waved it in the air. Maybe he was talking to his estranged family.

She shuffled into the kitchen and poured herself a glass of orange juice. Holding her breath, she glanced at her fully charged phone. No more messages from the dead.

Of course, Chris hadn't been dead when he sent that message—not yet anyway—and she hadn't forgotten about the mysterious code word. *Tempest.*

She charged toward her office and retrieved her laptop. When she powered it on, she groaned at the blue screen mocking her. She'd been having problems with her computer ever since she moved here. The tech guy on the mainland told her it might happen again, and if it did, she'd need to bring it back. No chance of that now.

Her gaze darted to the side where Jase's laptop glowed invitingly. No blue screens there. She strolled toward the invitation.

He did have password protection, but she'd seen him enter it last night—Semper Fi—all lowercase and no spaces. How could she forget that?

Resting her fingers on the keyboard, she watched Jase outside, still on the phone. He wouldn't mind if she looked up *tempest* on his laptop, would he?

She was surprised he hadn't jumped on that himself. He'd seemed more intrigued by the word that linked Lou and Chris than she was. She knew he'd been up early this morning to retrieve the Kleinschmidts' boat, so maybe he had already looked it up and didn't tell her because he hadn't found anything.

She launched his web browser, which automatically displayed a search engine. She entered the word *tempest*.

The expected and the unexpected popped up—references to Shakespeare's play, a dictionary definition of the word, a video game and even an actress's name. She continued to page through the findings, but didn't discover anything ominous about the word—no new drug, nothing illegal, no secret society.

What had it meant to Lou and then Chris? Was it something that had signed their death warrants? Would it sign hers?

She bit her lip and switched to her email provider. Scrolling through her email, she deleted the junk and saved the queries from her website for estimates. Getting Moonstones up and running was going to take longer than she expected. She might as well see if she could pick up a few decorating jobs in the meantime, even if it meant a few quick trips down to LA.

She patted her stomach. She'd be good to fly for the next few months.

She closed out of everything and zeroed in on a file called *Book* on Jase's desktop. Could it be that easy?

She hunched over the table to look out the window. Jase had ended his call, but was busy measuring from one post to another.

Feeling guilty and sneaky, but very excited, she double-clicked on the file. It opened and her mouth opened with it.

One sentence glared back at her and sent a chill up her spine. She whispered the words. "'It was a dark and stormy night and a tempest was headed for Break Island.'"

With her hand trembling, she closed out of the file and slammed the laptop shut and then remembered that he'd left it open. She opened it again with a sinking feeling. She hadn't made any changes to the file, but would the computer record that someone had opened it?

Too late now.

She raised her eyes to Jase working in her yard. Who was he? That couldn't be his entire book, could it? She felt like the wife in that scary movie with Jack Nicholson when she'd read pages and pages of the same phrase over and over again in her husband's tome.

A shattering noise from the front yard made her jump back from the window. Jase had split a cord of wood with an ax. Jack Nicholson's character in the movie had an ax, too.

Crossing her arms, she backed away from the computer and the window. She retreated to the kitchen, her eyes flicking toward the laptop. Maybe that file didn't represent his book. Maybe his book was in a folder somewhere else.

She hadn't even checked when he'd last saved the file. Maybe he was just playing with a new idea based on all the stuff going on since his arrival on the island. The sentence itself was a joke, not a serious attempt at writing.

She paced while hugging herself, the flannel pajamas no longer warm enough. She'd snooped and paid the price.

If she confronted him about it, she'd have to admit she'd accessed his laptop on the sly. If she didn't confront him, she'd have to continue to suspect his motives—and his sanity—just as with Simon.

She heard him stomping his boots on the porch and took the best course of action. She retreated to the rooms in the back and cranked on the shower. After locking the door.

The warm water calmed her nerves. She hadn't stumbled on his book. Jase Buckley didn't pose any threat to her. He'd saved her on the water and had been there for her when Lou had attacked her and then wound up dead on the deck. He'd come to her defense when he thought Chris Kitchens meant to do her harm and then had insisted on accompanying her when Chris texted her his warnings.

Jase was one of the good guys.

She finished her shower and dressed in the bathroom. When she entered the sitting room, Jase turned from staring out the window, his hand resting on his open laptop.

Keeping her eyes pinned to his face, she asked, "Did you get a lot of work done this morning? The fence is looking pretty good."

"What?"

"The fence." He knew. He knew she'd been snooping.

"Oh, yeah. Coming along, and I picked up the boat." He swung his head back toward the window. "Did you have breakfast? I was kind of hoping for more blueberry pancakes."

"I was…busy."

He turned to face her, his gaze raking her from head to toe. "Taking a shower? You must've slept in. That's good. Did you sleep well?"

"Yes, because…" She closed her eyes and dragged her fingers through her damp hair. "I went onto your laptop."

His eyebrows jumped. "I have a password."

"I saw you enter your password last night before I went to bed."

"Why did you use my computer?"

His soft voice made her swallow. "M-mine is corrupted and I wanted to search for *tempest*."

"Did you find it?"

"I found— No, I didn't find out anything about that word." She twisted her fingers in front of her. "I found your book. *Is* that your book?"

"That's it."

His flat admission sent adrenaline surging through her body and she flung her arms out to her sides and took a step back. "I don't understand."

"I'm not Jase Buckley, Nina, and I'm not a writer. I'm Jase Bennett and I'm an agent for an undercover ops organization—just like Simon was."

Chapter Fifteen

Her arms fell to her sides. She took another step back. Why did she attract the lunatics? She'd had this man in her bed, in her heart.

She folded her arms over her baby bump. No wonder he'd reminded her of Simon. Two sides of the same crazy coin. Jase had done a much better job of disguising his madness, though.

"Jase, I think you'd better leave now."

His dark eyes widened and he threw back his head and laughed.

She jumped.

"I thought you'd be angry with me, maybe throw something at me—but you just think I'm crazy."

"I don't think that." She shook her head back and forth, her hair whipping from side to side. "Not at all. But I think it's time you left and did your covert ops stuff somewhere else."

He reached behind his back. She ducked.

The look on his face gave her pause—gave her hope. He held his hands in front of him, clutching a thumb drive. "Don't be afraid, Nina. I know it sounds crazy to you, but it's the truth. I would've told you sooner, but I wasn't supposed to reveal my identity to you or tell you what was going on until…until a later date. But with everything going on—Lou, Chris, Tempest—we need to tell you."

"Don't be afraid? You ask me not to be afraid and then bring up Lou and Chris?" She jabbed her finger at him. "What's that?"

"Proof." He pulled out the chair in front of the laptop. "It's proof that everything I'm saying is true. Have a seat. I don't bite."

He'd used the same phrase she'd used on him last night when inviting him to join her in bed. Was it deliberate? She studied his face, and his mouth turned up at one corner.

A little bit of tension seeped from between her shoulder blades and she walked to the chair. She sat on the corner of it, gripping the edge of the table.

Jase leaned over her to insert the thumb drive into the side of the laptop, and her shoulders stiffened.

"Sorry about this." He moved the cursor to the Book file and deleted it. "It was my attempt to add some humor to our situation."

"Our situation."

"You're not in this alone, Nina. I've always been on your side."

A man this sincere couldn't be a whack job, could he? But the alternative he was proposing wasn't much better.

He opened the thumb drive, which was populated with multiple folders. "I'm really not supposed to be sharing this with you, but you deserve to know what's going on and I've kept you in the dark long enough."

He double-clicked on a folder, and she held her breath. If this folder contained more of his bizarre attempts at writing a book, she was ready to sprint.

Instead, a photo of her on the phone and getting into her car on the street in front of her LA condo filled the computer screen. She jerked her head to the side. "How did you get this?"

He clicked the mouse and another picture of her appeared and another and another, all going about her daily business.

She gasped, half out of her chair. "You were following me in LA?"

"Not me personally. I don't do surveillance like this."

The photos were professional, taken with a high-powered telephoto lens. There's no way she wouldn't have noticed someone that close taking a picture of her. But maybe she sensed the scrutiny.

"What *do* you do?

"I'm on the personal security end. My job right now is to protect targets."

"I'm a target? Why?"

He closed out her personal photo album and opened another folder. Some sort of document or report flashed on the screen with Simon's picture prominently displayed in the middle.

She covered her mouth with one hand. "You knew all about Simon."

He tapped the monitor. "Probably more than you did. Simon Skinner was a covert ops agent, like me, but for a different agency."

Her eyes scanned details of Simon's life, including a map pinpointing his locations over the past few years.

She squinted at the red dots. She knew he'd traveled a lot for his so-called government security job, but she had no idea he'd traveled to Yemen, Beijing, Libya.

She slumped back in her chair. Jase couldn't be just a garden-variety nut job with all this info and high tech at his fingertips, but that meant he was telling the truth. She didn't know which frightened her more.

"When you say covert ops agency, do you mean the CIA?"

"Both of our agencies are offshoots of the CIA. The average citizen has never heard the names and is unaware of our activities."

"Who *is* aware of your activities?"

"It's on a need-to-know basis—sometimes the military, sometimes the CIA, sometimes the president."

"Only *sometimes* for the president?"

"Do you believe me now? The book was just a cover to take me to Break Island."

"Why are you here? Just because I'm Simon Skinner's ex-fiancée? Was I right all along? Is he the one stalking me? And because he's one of these secret agents, you guys had to get involved?"

"It's more complicated than that, Nina. It's Tempest."

She slammed her palms down on each side of the laptop. "What's Tempest? What is it? You know, don't you? That's why you got so freaked out when I showed you that slip of paper from Lou's pocket."

His broad chest expanded as he filled his lungs with air. When he'd released the last bit of breath, he double-clicked another folder. An image of dark, swirling clouds took over the screen and an unaccountable feeling of dread thrummed through her system.

"Simon worked for Tempest. It's one of the covert ops agencies I was talking about."

"Then it is Simon following me. He has something to do with the deaths of Lou and Chris. That's why they knew about Tempest."

"It's not Simon, Nina."

"How do you know that? How can you be so sure?"

"Nina." He crouched beside her chair and took both of

her hands in his, still rough with dirt from his work outside. "Simon's dead."

"No." Her belly flip-flopped. "He can't be dead."

"He is. I'm sorry, Nina. I'm sorry I couldn't tell you before. It's been hell listening to you voice your suspicions about him, knowing all the time how false they were."

She snatched her hands away from his. "You're lying."

"I'm not lying, Nina."

A laugh bubbled up from her throat and she jumped up from the chair, knocking it over. "Because you've been so honest about everything else?"

"I had no choice in the matter. We're talking national security issues."

She drove a thumb into her chest. "I have something to do with national security?"

"You do now."

She paced away from him, her hands settling on her stomach. "How did he die? When did he die?"

He ran his hands across his face and for the first time she noticed the deep lines on both sides of his tight mouth. "I'm telling you this because he was your fiancé, because you're carrying his baby and because your life may be in danger because of that."

Her heart fluttered in her chest and for a brief moment she wanted to run away and pull the covers over her head, but this was Will's father, a story she might well have to tell her son someday.

"What happened to him? Is it related to his PTSD?"

"It's related to his behavior but Simon didn't have PTSD."

"What did he have? Why did he go off the deep end like that?"

"He'd been drugged, programmed, and in trying to break free from the mind control, he lost his mind."

Her body swayed as if she was on the deck of a sailboat, and Jase was immediately at her side. "Sit down. Do you need some water?"

He led her to the love seat where they'd been so close last night in front of the fire. And all along he'd known these terrible truths about Simon, her baby's father.

She sank into the cushion, and Jase returned with two glasses of water. She downed half of hers with one gulp.

"Are you telling me that Tempest did that to him?"

"Not just to Simon. We have reason to believe that Tempest had all of its agents on the same program. They're still on it. Simon was one of the strong ones. They could never completely control him, and when he and another agent figured out what Tempest was doing to them, they went rogue."

"Another agent?"

"He's the one who came in from the field and told us this story. We had plenty of reasons to doubt him, but everything he's claimed has checked out."

"Max Duvall."

His hand jerked and he spilled his water all over the front of his flannel shirt. "How do you know that name?"

"I met him once. He came to our condo when our relationship was on the precipice. Simon introduced him as a coworker and then they went outside to talk."

"That's the agent."

She nodded. "You still haven't told me what happened to Simon."

He looked away and cleared his throat.

"It's bad, isn't it?"

"He died, Nina. He died as a result of what those bastards did to him. He died trying to break free from the yoke of servitude that Tempest imposed on him."

"Why is Tempest doing this to its agents?"

"According to Duvall, Tempest is creating a cadre of

superagents—strong, invincible, impervious to pain, devoid of conscience."

"That's crazy." She dipped her fingers in her water glass and rubbed her temples with the cool moisture. "It's like science fiction."

"That's why it took a while to verify Duvall's story."

"But why me? Why did you land on my doorstep?"

Jase wiped his hands on the seat of his pants. "I told you. I'm the protector. I came here to watch over you."

"Why would Tempest care about me? Simon told me nothing about his work. I obviously didn't even know the name of his agency."

"We're not sure. My boss had an intuition about you and sent me out here."

"To pose as a writer-handyman."

"That's right."

"And it seems that your boss's intuition was correct. Tempest is here. Tempest is watching me. Tempest was watching me in LA. You both were. No wonder I felt stalked."

"I don't know how they contacted Lou and I don't know how Chris found out about them, but it's clear they had a hand in their deaths." He scratched the stubble on his chin. "And your boat accident."

"What?" She choked on her last sip of water. "The boat?"

"The first day I met you. We both assumed Lou was responsible for damaging your boat, but she never admitted it. Why not? She'd admitted everything else."

"You think Tempest put a hole in my boat?"

"Yeah."

"For what purpose?"

"To scare you, put you on edge. They don't know you or this area. Maybe they thought that would be enough to drown you, but if they wanted to kill you, I think they would've done so by now."

She pushed up from the love seat. "That's a lovely thought. What now?"

"I need to get you out of here, off this island. My agency can offer you refuge."

"I think it's a little too late for that."

"Why do you say that?"

As if to punctuate her point, a flash of lightning lit up the room and a rumble of thunder shook the floor.

"Nobody's getting off this island."

Chapter Sixteen

Jase flung open the front door and stepped onto the porch. The dark clouds that had been threatening from a distance all morning had moved in swiftly to envelop the island. A gust of wind slammed against the house, ripping off the shutter that had been hanging by a thread.

Backing up, he stepped over the threshold and clicked the door shut on the encroaching storm. "That came in fast."

"Not really," Nina called from the kitchen, where she'd put on the kettle for hot water. "The weather guy on TV has been forecasting it all week. All the signs were there."

He strode to the kitchen. "Why don't you sit down? You've had a huge shock this morning. If you give me directions, I can try to replicate those pancakes from yesterday."

She kept her back to him and hunched her shoulders as she braced her hands against the stove. "You can stop now, Jason Bennett."

Uh-oh. He had a feeling he'd been experiencing the calm before the storm when he told her about Simon and Tempest...and his own deception.

He wedged his shoulder against the wall. "Stop what? And everyone calls me Jase anyway."

She snorted. "At least that wasn't a lie."

"I thought you understood why I had to lie." Folding his arms, he dug his fingers into his biceps.

"Of course." She flicked her fingers in the air. "National security."

"We didn't have all the facts, Nina."

The whistle on the kettle blew, piercing the thick air between them. She grabbed the handle and dumped the boiling water over her tea bag in the cup and then jumped back as drops of water must've splashed up and scalded her wrist.

He shrugged off the wall and then stopped as she turned with her cup in hand, her blue eyes blazing. "You can stay here because it's going to start pouring rain in the next thirty minutes, but you don't have to pretend to care about me and the baby anymore."

"Pretend? There was no pretense on my part."

Biting her lip, she moved away from the stove and squeezed past him, holding her steaming cup aloft. She stopped at her office door and turned. "Was there ever really a pregnant girlfriend? A baby lost?"

His stomach dropped. "Good God, Nina. Do you really think I'd lie about that?"

"I think you'd lie about anything to do your job, which was get close to me and find out what I knew about Tempest."

"Tempest?" He ran a hand along his jaw. "We didn't think you knew anything about Tempest. It was always just about protecting you, making sure Tempest didn't come after you."

"I know. I got that part and now that I know all about Tempest and…and Simon, you can just do your job. You don't have to fake affection for me or my baby."

"Nina…"

The office door slammed and then shook for good measure.

He shoved his hands into his pockets and kicked at the leg of a chair. If it had been up to him, he would've told her when Lou died and she found that piece of paper in her stepsister's pocket, but Coburn had just given him the okay to tell her. The tremor in her voice and her glistening eyes told him she felt more hurt than angry.

Maybe he should've never gotten personal. Would she be this upset if he'd remained the handyman? Now she believed he'd held her and kissed her just to fake her out and let him in.

She couldn't be more wrong.

The wind howled outside and he felt like howling along with it.

He hunched over the counter, surveying the kitchen and weighing his options. Cereal. Instant oatmeal if she had it.

He glanced at the office door, firmly closed in his face. He'd look for it himself.

He grabbed a bowl from the cupboard and almost dropped it when someone started banging on the front door.

He shoved his weapon in the back of his waistband and put his eye to the peephole. Mr. Kleinschmidt, the single piece of gray hair on his head standing straight up, swayed on the porch.

Jase inched open the door so that it wouldn't be snatched from his grasp. "Mr. Kleinschmidt, what are you doing out here? You look ready to blow away."

He braced a gnarled hand on the post. "Like my boat?"

"Your boat?" The wind blew the rain sideways and soaked Mr. Kleinschmidt's jacket. Jase grabbed his arm and pulled him inside. "What about your boat?"

Nina had wandered in from the sealed fortress of her office, her eyes wide. "What's going on? The storm has really picked up, hasn't it?"

"It snatched my boat right from the dock." Mr. Kleinschmidt ran a hand over his wet face.

"How did that happen? It was tied up." Jase stalked to the window to peek outside. The Kleinschmidts' boat had, indeed, vacated the dock.

"That's what I was going to ask you. We haven't taken it out since you brought it back early this morning. Did you secure it?"

"Of course."

"Did you see the boat out on the water, Carl?"

"It's gone, Nina."

She shot a gaze toward Jase. "Maybe someone stole it, maybe someone desperate to get to the mainland."

"We may have been desperate to get to the mainland. I think we just lost our last chance."

"Is the Harbor Patrol still letting boats cross?"

"I think this morning would've been our last opportunity."

Jase spread his hands. "I'm sorry, Mr. Kleinschmidt. I don't know what could've happened."

But he had a hollow feeling in the pit of his stomach. He had no doubt someone from Tempest was on the island and could even be responsible for the theft of the Kleinschmidts' boat. This agent had made contact with both Lou and Chris somehow. What he couldn't quite grasp is what he and Tempest wanted with Nina.

If the agency wanted her dead, she'd be dead. They could've targeted her in LA before Prospero even had her in its sights, before he'd taken up the job of protecting her.

And if they'd taken the trouble of punching a hole in Nina's boat, they could've just as easily packed it with explosives. He clenched his teeth and took a shuddering breath.

"Were you and Mrs. Kleinschmidt planning on evacuating the island?"

"Not now." Mr. Kleinschmidt tugged his damp jacket around him. "You know, Nina, the water's getting pretty high out there. The Harbor Patrol just might tell us coastal folks to move to higher ground."

"Would they do that?" Jase turned to Nina, whose pale face caused knots to form in his gut. Had the missing boat raised her suspicions, too?

Maybe he should've kept his secrets. He could've explained away the Book file, made a joke of it. He had enough legitimate reasons to protect her that had nothing to do with Tempest. She'd been buying his story up until this point. Now she was needlessly worried about something out of her control...but not out of his.

She twisted a lock of hair around her finger. "It happened once when I was a teenager. Am I remembering that right, Carl?"

"It was about ten years ago, and I think this monster storm has that one beat."

An evacuation would definitely complicate things. Jase asked, "How does the Harbor Patrol notify you if there's an evacuation?"

Mr. Kleinschmidt scratched his chin. "If they can't get out on the water, they'll come door-to-door and you'd better obey or they'll come down on you with fines. Maybe Dora and I can ride with you in the truck if it comes to that, Nina."

"Of course we'll give you and Dora a lift, Carl, and I'm sorry about the boat. I don't understand what could've happened. Do you think the wind was strong enough to snap the rope?"

"It might be in an hour or two, but it wasn't that bad this morning."

"Maybe the Harbor Patrol will find it on the bay."

"Maybe. You two take care now. Dora's going to want to help you out with the baby, Nina. She's been after me to move to California to be closer to the grandkids, so she can use yours as a substitute in the meantime."

So, she hadn't been fooling the Kleinschmidts at all. "That would be lovely. Do you need Jase to help you get back home?"

He waved them off. "Naw."

"I wanna have a look at the bay anyway. I'll walk back with you." Jase grabbed the mackinaw from last night and winked at Nina.

As soon as he stepped onto the porch, the rain lashed his face. He grabbed on to Mr. Kleinschmidt's arm, and the older man listed to the side.

He kept a firm grip on Mr. Kleinschmidt all the way to his front door, where his wife was hovering.

Then he turned toward their boat dock. The water churned and gurgled. Waves formed and crashed against the beach, the wind carrying the salty spray inland.

Even the current force of the water and wind weren't enough to rip a boat from its moorings. Either someone had untied it with the intent of letting it get carried away, or someone had stolen it.

And he hadn't noticed a thing. There was a lot he hadn't noticed since falling under the spell of Nina Moore.

He crouched and studied the area around the dock. Indentations from footprints crisscrossed the dirt and sand. They could belong to anyone.

He returned to Moonstones, and the closed office door. What was she doing in there? Her computer didn't even work.

He sat at his own computer and stared out the window at the darkening sky, which made the afternoon look like midnight.

He brought up his email and clicked on one from Jack. He'd sent a minidossier on Chris Kitchens and the guy was legit—dead but legit. So how had he run afoul of Tempest?

If Break Island had truly been a small town, without all the tourists and the mainlanders coming and going, it would've been a hell of a lot easier to zero in on a stranger. As it was, Nina didn't know half of the people she ran into on a daily basis.

A few hours later, after no communication from Nina, no food and an increasing deluge outside, the table lamp flickered and died. His laptop made a buzzing noise and went black.

Nina flew out of the office. "We lost power."

"Flashlights? Candles? You already mentioned you didn't have a generator."

"I'm not even sure about candles."

They both jumped when a voice boomed from a loud-speaker outside.

"This is the Snohomish County Sheriff's Department calling for an evacuation. Leave your homes on the coast and head over the dunes into town."

"The Kleinschmidts." Nina made for the front door and barreled down the porch.

By the time Jase joined her, she was already hanging on the door of the sheriff's truck and turned at his approach. "There's an evacuation center in the school gym. The school sits on a hill behind the main street."

"I've seen it."

The sheriff jerked his thumb over his shoulder. "You folks need to get going. The water's rising and churning and we're expecting some big waves and flooding. The road's going to be washed out for sure by the end of the day, and then you'll be completely cut off."

"Maybe the storm will level this place and I can start from scratch." Nina tossed her head back toward Moonstones.

"You might get your wish, but you don't want to be inside when it happens."

"We need to pick up the neighbors." Jase gestured to the Kleinschmidts' house.

"Yeah, the old guy opened the front door and waved. They heard us."

"We'll get going, then." Jase smacked the roof of the vehicle. "Thanks."

As Nina picked her way over the soggy ground to the Kleinschmidts' house, Jase held her arm whether she liked it or not.

Mr. Kleinschmidt swung open the door before they took their first step onto the porch.

"I heard, I heard. This storm's coming in like a son of a bitch."

"Carl?"

"It's Nina and her friend."

"Her fiancé?" Dora Kleinschmidt joined her husband at the door, carrying enough jackets to outfit a small army.

The fiancé and pregnancy story must've spread far and wide, because Mrs. Kleinschmidt studied him from behind a pair of thick glasses that magnified her eyes to scary proportions.

"Dora, this is Jason. Buckley—my fiancé."

Jase returned Mrs. Kleinschmidt's surprisingly strong grip. "Call me Jase. Everyone calls me Jase."

"Okay, enough with the introductions. You'll have hours to grill him at the school gym, Dora." Mr. Kleinschmidt took an armful of jackets from his wife.

Nina held up her finger. "Wait here. We'll get the rest of our stuff and drive the truck up to your gate."

They returned to the B and B and Nina collected a few items while Jase packed up his laptop and his weapon and stuffed them into a backpack.

Before she locked up, Nina paused on the threshold and gazed into the sitting room. "I almost do hope the place is destroyed. I need a fresh start."

He took the keys from her hand. "I'll drive."

They picked up Carl and Dora and crawled along the road to town with the rain falling so fast and furious the windshield wipers couldn't keep up.

They hit a little traffic jam winding onto the main street as other coastal residents had gotten the same directive from the sheriff's department.

As Jase pulled into a packed parking lot, he said, "I'll drop you all off at the entrance to the gym and then park the truck."

By the time he parked and slogged his way back through the school parking lot to the gym, Nina and the Kleinschmidts had claimed one corner of a few low bleacher rows.

Jase shed his jacket and hung it over a bleacher railing. "At least they keep it warm in here."

Mr. Kleinschmidt snorted. "With all these bodies in here it's going to get plenty warm."

"The Emersons are over by the coffee." Mrs. Kleinschmidt placed a hand on Nina's arm. "Do you mind if we leave you to say hello, Nina? I'm sure you two would like some time alone anyway."

"Of course not. It looks like they're getting a card game going, too. You might as well enjoy yourself."

Mrs. Kleinschmidt patted her arm. "You have this big, strong man to look out for you now."

Nina managed a tight smile.

When the Kleinschmidts crossed the room to join the card game, Jase puffed out a breath. "Thanks for not blowing my cover."

"What am I supposed to say? 'Jason Bennett is actually a spy for some black ops agency. Oh, and my ex-fiancé was one, too.'"

"I told you a lot more than you needed to know, Nina."

She rounded on him, her nostrils flaring. "You didn't

tell me nearly enough, Jase—you or Simon. I sensed the two of you were alike from the minute I met you."

"What do you want to know, Nina?"

"I want to know what that agency did to Simon. What kinds of things did they make him do? What happened to him at the end? Are they just drugging agents or are they up to something else?"

He pinched the bridge of his nose and squeezed his eyes shut. "Definitely something else."

She straddled the bleacher bench and dug her fingernails into his thigh. "Tell me, Jase. I'm having Simon's baby. We deserve to know."

He blew out a long breath. Jack Coburn didn't have to know everything. "I told you there was drugging and mind control going on. What Tempest hoped to accomplish, what we've heard anyway, is that Tempest has created a sort of superagent—strong, fearless, impervious to pain and impervious to their consciences. They sent them on assignments and then erased all memory of those assignments from their minds."

She covered her mouth, her blue eyes swimming with tears. "That's what they did to Simon?"

He took her hands and smoothed his thumb across her knuckles. "I'm sorry."

She disengaged one hand and clutched her belly. "The baby. Simon must've been on these drugs when I conceived."

"Yeah, it had been going on for over a year." He drew his brows over his nose, an unnamed dread forming in his gut. "What are you getting at, Nina?"

"What if those drugs had some effect on Will? What if my baby is in danger?"

Chapter Seventeen

"No." He placed both hands on her stomach, as if he could prevent any harm to Will. "Everything's fine, isn't it? I mean, you've had ultrasounds and an amniocentesis and all that?"

"I've had a few ultrasounds. I'm not old enough to warrant an amnio, but I need one now."

She needed to stop this line of thought. He couldn't handle another lost baby. Will had to be okay.

He took her face between his hands. "Will's fine. Everything's going to be fine. When this storm is over, I'm going to take you away from here, someplace safe. We'll get the best doctors in the world to look after you."

"So, you *do* think something might be wrong."

"Not at all."

She blinked. Then her eyes widened and she whispered, "You'll never guess who's coming up behind you."

He dropped his hands and craned his head over his shoulder.

Kip Chandler, as scruffy as ever, stopped a few feet away and raised his hand in a peace sign. "Okay to approach, man?"

Jase swung his leg over the bench and turned to face him. "You have a lot of people looking for you."

Kip scooped his dishwater-blond hair back from his

forehead. "I figured that. I've already checked in with the cops. Told them I couldn't handle the heat after...after." He dipped his head, cupping a hand over his eyes.

Hunching forward, Jase asked, "So, you knew what had happened to Lou before you took off?"

"I told her to slow down, and then I left. I heard later that she probably OD'd."

Nina crooked her finger at him. "Tell us what happened that night. Do you know about Chris, the redhead we were with?"

He plopped on the floor beside them, crossing his legs. "I heard. Even more reason for me to lay low."

"Why are you still on the island?" Jase narrowed his eyes. He'd have to check with the chief to make sure he knew Kip was back. He didn't trust the guy. "We figured you'd taken off."

"I wanted to. I didn't have the dough. I've been hiding out. There are a lot of places to hide out on this island."

"Did you have anything to do with Lou's death?" Nina crossed her arms, and Jase was almost grateful to Kip for getting Nina's mind off the baby.

"No way. We'd had a few and we smoked a blunt, shared it with Red. I didn't know Lou had any of the hard stuff. Red left and Lou and I crashed at the motel. I woke up alone, heard what happened and went underground. I can't afford to have cops sniffing around me."

"Do you know where Lou got the hard stuff? The EMTs thought it might be heroin?"

Nina was like a dog with a bone.

Kip held up a pair of dirty hands. "I have no clue. Maybe Red had it. He didn't seem to be any stranger to the drug culture."

One of the volunteers came by with some bottles of water. "Anyone thirsty? It's going to be a long night. We're putting out sandwiches in a few minutes, too."

"Thanks. We'll have two waters." Jase picked up two bottles with one hand.

"Make that three." Kip snatched one from the tray.

Jase rolled his eyes at Nina. He sure as hell hoped Kip didn't plan to camp out with them all night. To discourage him, Jase reached for his backpack and pulled out his laptop.

Kip leveled a finger at the computer. "You working on your book?"

Who told him about the book? Jase slid a glance at Nina, who ignored him while she twisted off the cap from her bottle of water. "Yeah."

"I got some stories for you, man."

"I'm sure you do, Kip, but this one's about my experiences in Afghanistan." Jase lowered himself to the floor, stretched his legs in front of him and leaned against the bottom of the bleachers.

After several minutes of Nina grilling Kip about Lou, she raised her head. "They're putting some food out. Do you want me to get you something?"

Jase lifted his laptop. "I'll get it."

Nina had already jumped to her feet. "You're all settled. I need to stretch my legs, anyway."

A sudden fear gripped the back of his neck. "Don't go outside."

"Why would I do that? The storm's coming at us in full force."

Kip rose to his feet. "I could use some food, but I'd better wash my hands first."

"The bathrooms are through those doors by where the food is set up."

Kip ambled after Nina across the gym and Jase kept his eye on both of them. Kip hadn't had any serious offenses on his rap sheet, but the dude was no angel.

Nina returned first with four wrapped sandwiches, two

bags of chips and a couple of apples. "It's not Mandy's fish-and-chips, but the sandwiches look pretty good."

Jase took a paper plate from her, unwrapped two sandwiches and put them on the plate. He chugged some water and put the bottle on the floor next to the plate.

Kip came back, munching on an apple. "I already wolfed down one sandwich. My meals have been a little sketchy, so that hit the spot.

"Are you going to read us any of your book?" Kip came in close to Jase and leaned over his laptop. Then his foot hit Jase's bottle of water and it fell across his plate, soaking his sandwiches.

"Sorry, man." Kip jumped back from the puddle. "Let me get you some paper towels and a couple more sandwiches."

"That's all right." Jase scooted away from the water on the floor. Were they ever going to get rid of this guy?

As if reading his thoughts or maybe just his expression, Kip said, "No, really. I'll drop off your sandwiches and go find a place to hole up in here and get some sleep. I'm hoping the ferry will be giving free rides back to the mainland tomorrow or whenever this storm lets up."

Jase watched Kip cross the room and turned to Nina. "What do you think about Kip's story?"

"I'm not sure. You?"

He tapped his wrist. "He had his sleeves rolled up, so I glanced at his arms and he doesn't have any track marks or anything. Plus, he looks too buff to be into those hard drugs."

"Kip? Buff?"

"He had his sweatshirt unzipped, too, and he's got some muscle there."

"If you say so."

He didn't want her worrying about any of this. Brushing her cheek with one knuckle, he whispered, "How are you doing?"

"I'm doing just fine, but if you think I've forgotten about what those drugs could've been doing to my baby, you're wrong."

"Nina."

"I told you, Jase. You don't have to pretend to care about us anymore."

"And I told you…"

"Sandwiches." Kip handed Jase two wrapped sandwiches on a plate. "I also picked up a blanket, so I'm going to try to get some shut-eye."

Kip wandered away, the blanket pinned between his arm and the side of his body.

Nina heaved a sigh. "Let's just leave this alone, Jase. I'm not embarrassed to admit that I felt something for you, but now I realize it was all fake."

"I was here under false pretenses, but that has nothing to do with how I feel about you."

She put down her sandwich. "And how is that? Protective because it's your job? Protective because Maggie lost your baby?"

He put a finger to her lips and then replaced it with his own lips.

She resisted his attempts at a kiss by sealing her lips, but when he ran a hand along her throat and cupped one full breast in his palm, she sighed and her lips softened beneath his.

He deepened the kiss until she made squeaking noises.

He pulled away. "You don't like that?"

"I like it a lot, but we're in the middle of a gym with hundreds of other evacuees."

He picked up his sandwich and took a huge bite, his appetite surging back. "Nobody noticed a thing—besides, aren't we engaged?"

She nibbled on the edge of her sandwich. "One kiss is not going to make me forget that you lied to me and kept Simon's death from me."

"I know, Nina, but look at it this way. Simon was in the same line of work, and he kept it all from you. He lied to you every day. He had to. He did it to keep you safe."

She sniffled and ripped a piece of crust from her bread. "He didn't do a very good job, did he?"

"He did his best." He demolished the rest of his sandwich and finished off his second one, too.

She held up a blanket. "Unless they also plan to show a movie tonight, I'm going to try to get some sleep."

"I'll put my laptop on the bench." He patted his lap. "Put your head here and tuck that blanket around you."

"Aren't you sleeping?"

He gazed around the gym, cluttered with people, some he'd seen before in the shops and businesses and along the wharf and some he'd never laid eyes on in his life.

"I'm going to stay awake, keep watch."

She spread out one blanket on the polished wood and curled up on her side, resting her head on his thighs.

He tugged the other blanket around her and whispered, "When you wake up, this will all be over. The storm will pass."

THE THUNDER BOOMED, shaking the floor beneath him. Jase blinked as cold water splashed on his face. His stomach turned.

He opened his eyes and tried to focus on the ceiling. Where was he?

Several drops of water hit him and rolled down his cheeks. He gagged as his gut churned.

The gym. They had been evacuated to the school gym. God, he felt nauseous. He dropped his chin to his chest, his neck stiff and sore, his mouth dry—until it wasn't.

He rubbed the back of his neck, and several more drops of water splashed onto his head. He looked up into the recesses of the ceiling. The roof of the gym must have a leak.

As his mouth watered, he brought his knees to his chest. He was going to vomit. Was it the sandwiches? Was Nina sick, too?

He glanced down, but Nina was gone. His head jerked up and he scanned the darkened gym. Shapes huddled around the floor of the gym, a few flashlights and penlights punctuated the gloom and low conversations hummed in the night.

Where did Nina go? He knew pregnant women had to pee a lot, so maybe she'd headed to the restroom.

That's where he needed to be if his stomach wouldn't stop roiling and churning. He didn't want to throw up on the gym floor.

He stretched and reached for his almost-empty bottle of water and nearly knocked it over when his laptop beeped at him. The screen saver flashed and flickered, and he brushed his fingers across the touchpad to wake it up and log in.

A red square pulsated on the display, indicating he had an urgent message. He clicked on it, and an email from Coburn popped up on the screen.

He read the message once. He read the message twice.

Kip Chandler's body was found in a garbage dump. He'd been dead for two weeks. The man calling himself Kip Chandler is an imposter. I repeat. Kip Chandler is an imposter.

Chapter Eighteen

The cold rain lashed her face and the wind plucked at her ponytail, yanking strands loose and plastering them against her wet cheeks. "Where are you taking me? We can't go anywhere in this storm."

The man with Kip pressed the barrel of his gun against the small of her back. "Stop talking."

She threw a beseeching glance at Kip, walking by her side, gripping her arm. "Where are we going, Kip? What's this all about?"

She didn't want to show her hand and mention Simon or Tempest. "Is this about Lou? The cops aren't even looking for you. They've written it off as a drug overdose."

"Do be quiet, Nina. This bloke isn't kidding. He really wants you to shut up and he has no sense of humor."

Just as it had when she'd first heard it, Kip's English accent jolted her. Who the hell was he and how had he hooked up with Lou? Why had he hooked up with Lou?

She shook the rain from her face and shivered. She knew why—to get to her.

"Wh-what did you do to Jase? He wasn't just sleeping, was he?"

"I drugged his sandwiches."

The robot prodding her with the gun grunted. "Enough to kill him?"

"It should be."

Nina choked on a sob.

"You just never know with those bloody Prospero agents, do you?"

"Do you want me to make sure?"

"Maybe later. We need to get her to the warehouse."

"Warehouse?" The only warehouses she knew about were located on the pier. "Why are we going to a warehouse?"

Kip had grown tired of her, and the man with the gun had no intention of answering her questions.

She should've never gone off so willingly with Kip from the gym. With Jase sleeping soundly, Kip explained that he had more info about Lou and Chris but he suspected Jase of being an undercover cop.

Nothing she told Kip, or whoever he was, could convince him otherwise, so she'd left the gym with him only to be met by the goon with the gun.

The drugging of Jase terrified her but made sense. He wouldn't have abandoned his job by falling asleep. He wouldn't have abandoned her.

She said a silent prayer that someone would notice him and try to wake him. She felt sure that once awake, Jase would do anything to fight the effects of the drug.

She glanced at Kip, his shaggy hair slicked back to reveal sharp features. What did Tempest want with her? As Jase said, they could've killed her long ago. Kip and his henchman could've killed her outside the gym. Instead, they were marching her to some warehouse.

For what purpose? Torture? Would they try to find out what Simon had told her? They'd be sorely disappointed. She knew nothing.

She placed her hand on her tummy and patted, sending soothing vibes to Will.

"Don't worry about your baby, Nina. We're not going to hurt him."

Bitter bile rose in her throat and she spit it out, aiming for Kip's shoes. Even the fact that these people knew about her baby terrified her.

After relentlessly fighting the wind and slogging through puddles of water, they came upon the wharf. She'd been right about the warehouse.

Is this where Kip had been hiding out for the past few days?

The boats moored in their slips thrashed and bucked like wild horses in a stable. The row of abandoned warehouses huddled beyond the bait shop and they trudged toward them.

When they reached the last one, Kip produced a key for the shiny new lock and pulled the door open. He pushed her through first and she stumbled in the darkness.

"Be careful." He caught her arm and steadied her.

"That's a little ridiculous—coming from you."

He clicked his tongue. "We're here to take care of you, Nina, until the next stage of your journey."

Her wet flesh turned icy cold. What the hell was he talking about? "I don't understand any of this. Who are you? Is this some plan of Lou's?"

"That junkie?" He brushed his hands together. "She was just a means to an end—you. I have to say she proved to be more loyal to you than I expected. When I tried to convince her to get close enough to you so that I could kidnap you, she refused. Even after I offered her money. Of course, I would've taken that money back once I killed her, but she didn't know that."

Nina's throat burned with tears. "You killed her."

"I offered her some smack and she took it."

"And Chris Kitchens? What happened to him?"

"He snooped where he shouldn't have snooped, but you already knew that about him—nosy, intrusive."

He flipped on a lamp powered by a generator and she gasped and stepped back.

"What is all this?" Her gaze darted around the room, where Kip had created a cozy enclave—a bed, space heaters, a platter of cheese and fruit, a carafe of orange juice and one of milk.

"We're here to take care of you, Nina. I believe the storm will abate enough tomorrow morning so that we can leave."

Her heart slammed against her rib cage. "Leave? Where are we going?"

"To a secure location where we can nurture your baby until he's born."

Her knees buckled but Kip caught her. "You see? You need care."

"What are you? Who are you?"

"Let's get you settled."

She wrenched away from him. "I don't want to get settled here and I'm not going anywhere with you."

The guard dog loomed over her, brandishing his gun.

"You'll do what I say, Nina, or Zeke will make your life miserable."

Eyeing Zeke's gun and expressionless face, she asked, "What do you want me to do?"

"That's so much better for everyone." He plucked at the sleeve of her wet jacket. "Get out of these wet clothes and change into the nightgown across the bed."

She crossed her arms. "I'm not taking my clothes off."

"We're not here to molest you." He snapped his fingers, and Zeke yanked off her jacket. "Now, you can undress yourself and get into that nightgown or Zeke can undress you and perhaps accidently molest you."

She swallowed hard and then crept toward the bed. "Keep your backs turned toward me."

"So you can run off or do something equally stupid?" He followed her to the bed and cranked on all the space heaters. "I don't think so."

"I don't…"

One look from Kip and Zeke started stalking toward her.

"Okay, okay." She toed off her boots and peeled her wet socks from her feet. She rolled down her leggings and then turned her back as she pulled her sweater over her head. Wearing just her underwear, she reached for the nightgown.

"Everything." Kip threw a towel at her back. "Remove all your clothing. It's damp and we don't want you taking a chill."

With her underwear still in place, she toweled off. She kept the towel around her waist and slipped the nightgown over her head. Then she dropped the towel and shimmied out of her panties and bra.

Kip scooped up all her clothing and laid it out in front of one of the space heaters. "You can have your clothes back tomorrow morning or whenever we get out of here."

"How are you leaving the island? Do you have a boat?"

He ignored her while he hovered over the food.

She perched on the edge of the bed. "Are you going to tell me what's going on now?"

He poured a glass of milk and selected cheese and fruit to arrange on another plate. "Have your snack and we'll talk."

She took the plate from him and balanced it on her lap. This whole situation was creeping her out.

"Your prenatal vitamin." He shook a big white pill onto her plate.

"I already take them."

"Take these."

With trembling fingers she picked up the vitamin, or whatever it was, and dropped it onto her tongue. She took a sip of milk and lodged the pill in her cheek.

Before she could blink an eyelash, Zeke was in front of her, shoving his thick fingers into her mouth. He found the pill and held it up to Kip. Then he smacked her across the face.

Her head whipped to the side as Kip swore.

"Control yourself, Zeke." Kip handed her another vitamin. "Swallow the pill, Nina. They're just prenatal vitamins."

With her eyes watering, she gulped down the pill. "Why are you doing this?"

Kip poured himself a glass of juice. "Because you're carrying Simon Skinner's baby."

She shook her head. "I don't understand."

"Simon worked for us. I know you know that now because Jase Bennett told you. You also know Simon Skinner is dead. He went berserk in a lab and was killed by one of our other agents."

Nina covered her mouth with her hand. Jase had never told her how it happened.

"Simon Skinner was very special to us—until he rebelled." He rolled the glass between his hands. "He was one of our superagents, conditioned, prepped and primed—like Zeke here. Elite."

"It put him over the edge of madness."

"Only because he stopped taking the medication that made him special—but not before he impregnated you."

Her hands cupped her belly beneath the soft flannel of the nightgown. She and Jase had been following the wrong path. Tempest didn't believe the drugs Simon was taking were going to hurt her baby—just the opposite.

"What are you saying?"

"I can see by your face that you already understand, Nina. We believe your baby is genetically predisposed to all the qualities we want in an agent."

"That's crazy."

"Is it?" He nodded toward Zeke. "Let's take Zeke. He's a man, but a reconstituted one. He's special—stronger, heightened senses, oblivious to pain—perfect for our purposes, as your baby will be."

She stood up suddenly and the plate of food crashed to the floor. "You're not getting anywhere near my baby."

"We already are, Nina. We have him. He's ours and you're ours for the next…four months. We'll pamper you, make sure you have the best of everything, make sure the baby has the best of everything. Your position will be quite enviable."

"And once I've given birth?"

"A baby needs his mother. Breast-feeding is the best start to life, and your breast milk will be very special, Nina."

Nausea swept through her body and she broke into a cold sweat. These people were insane. They really believed they could turn her baby into some kind of super-baby they could groom into the perfect agent.

"I'm not going to be a party to this insanity."

"You no longer have a choice in the matter. Once this storm clears, we're going to whisk you away to a very secure and secret location. Nobody will be able to find us—not Jase Bennett, not fifty Prospero agents, not Jack Coburn himself."

Kip took a turn around the room, his face illuminated with an almost religious zeal. "Think of it, Nina. Your boy will be the first, our test subject. Once we meet with success, our agents can impregnate other strong women like you. Our superagents have no problem in that area at all—our special formula, T-101, makes them especially potent and virile. Didn't you find that with Simon?"

Lou's craziness didn't hold a candle to this guy's. She couldn't allow him to take her off the island. Once they left Break Island, it would be over for her, for Will. Their drugs would probably kill him.

She swooped down and grabbed a shard of glass from the plate and ran for the door of the warehouse. But Zeke was at the door before she got there and twisted her hand until she dropped the glass.

He lifted her in his arms as she beat against his chest and face, but she might as well have been fighting against a slab of granite. He deposited her back on the bed and held her while Kip secured her arms and legs with leather straps lined with sheepskin.

Looking down at her, Kip clicked his tongue. "I don't know why you have to make this so difficult. You belong to us now. Your son belongs to us. And there's not a damned thing Jase Bennett can do about it."

Chapter Nineteen

Jase shoved his fingers down his throat once more and vomited the last of the poison from his system. If that ceiling hadn't been leaking above him, waking him up with cold water on his face, he'd be out cold. Then he would've regurgitated in his sleep and choked on his own vomit. That's how it worked.

Kip, or whoever the hell he was, would be free and clear to remove Nina from the island, to kidnap her. He was convinced that's what Tempest wanted. Otherwise, Kip would've poisoned Nina's sandwich, too.

What did they want with her? What did they want with her baby?

Someone flushed a urinal. "You okay in there?"

"Yeah, just puking my guts out. I'll live."

"Hope it wasn't those sandwiches."

No, just *his* sandwiches.

He waited for the other man to leave the bathroom, and then he staggered to his feet, wiping his mouth with the back of his hand. He grabbed a wad of toilet paper and blew his nose.

He pushed out of the stall and hunched over the sink. He cranked on the cold water and splashed his face, filling his mouth and then rinsing and spitting over and over.

Gripping the edge of the porcelain, he leaned into the

wavy mirror. The distorted image that peered back at him matched the way he felt.

He headed back into the gym and grabbed two bottles of water. He downed the first one and twisted off the cap to the second. Almost all of the evacuees were sleeping while the storm raged outside.

Kip couldn't have left the island with Nina, even though it had been hours since Jase passed out. A boat would've never lasted out on that sound.

He sidled up next to a window, boarded over with plywood, and put his eye to the crack between the pieces of wood. The wind had died down a little and the blackness had faded to graphite gray.

A few more hours and dawn would break over the island. The storm would be on its way out. Would the Harbor Patrol allow boats to leave for the mainland?

Would Kip be foolish enough to launch a boat from the wharf, where anyone could see him? Where he could see him?

If Kip thought his poisoned sandwiches had been successful, he wouldn't be looking for Jase, but how would you get an unwilling pregnant woman onto a boat in the light of day?

Even if Kip knocked out Nina, drugged her, he'd have to carry her onto the boat. Too many people in this town knew Nina for Kip to get away with that.

He could take her from her own boat dock at Moonstones. Maybe he'd taken her back to Moonstones and they were there now waiting for the storm to pass. If Kip thought he'd killed his adversary, he wouldn't be worried about him showing up. He wouldn't be concerned about the Kleinschmidts stopping him, and there was no one else.

Jase felt a flare of hope. That made sense. Kip would take her to Moonstones, where he had a boat waiting for them—maybe even the Kleinschmidts' boat, which he'd stolen earlier.

His gaze traveled around the gym. He had to get out of here. He had to rescue Nina and Will.

Keeping close to the walls of the gym, he crossed to the other side where double doors led to a causeway connecting the gym to the rest of the school. The organizers of the evacuation had wanted everyone to stay out of the school, but nobody saw him as he slipped out one of the doors.

Rivers of water rushed down the causeway and swirled around the drains and vents that couldn't accommodate the deluge. Jase waded through the flood and turned the corner toward the parking lot. No cars had floated away, but nothing was drivable, either, as the water had reached as high as the wheel wells of the cars.

Had Kip and Nina walked out of here? They must have, unless Kip had stored a rowboat nearby.

He half walked, half slipped and slid down the hill to the main street, where windows had been boarded up and sandbags bunched up against the doors. The ankle-deep water slowed his progress, and when he got to the path that led to the other side of the dunes, he found a river of mud and sand.

He slogged through it all, one step at a time, convinced he'd find Nina at Moonstones.

The wind stopped howling for ten seconds and a streak of light pierced the horizon. Instead of filling him with encouragement, the abatement of the storm filled him with a terrible urgency. As soon as the storm broke and the dawn awakened, Kip would whisk Nina off the island.

If that happened, he would never find her. He'd never hold her again. He'd never have a chance to make love to her. He'd never look into her baby's face.

He pushed on, battling the water and the wind and his own guilt for allowing her to be snatched away from him.

When Moonstones appeared, not much worse for wear than before the storm, he almost dropped to his knees. Instead, he hunched forward, the sand dunes concealing him from prying eyes at the windows of the B and B.

He approached Moonstones from the deck side, where the bedraggled yellow crime scene tape flapped in the wind. Tempest had planned this abduction months ago. Kip Chandler had been targeted and murdered, his identity stolen, and then the fake Kip had insinuated himself into Lou Moore's life with booze and weed. It must've been laughably easy. Kip had probably convinced Lou to visit Nina for one more try at Moonstones, told her stories about his attorney brother and how he'd get the place back for her.

Tempest had found Nina's weak spot and had gone in for the kill. Literally. What had poor Lou discovered about Kip at the end? What had Chris discovered? If Chris had gotten wind that Kip knew anything about Simon, he would've done anything to get to the truth—even put himself in mortal danger.

From the deck, Jase peered out at the sound. His stomach dipped when he didn't see any boats at Nina's or the Kleinschmidts' docks. Nina's boat was still sitting on the trailer by the shed in the back.

Holding his gun in front of him, he slipped around to the front and peeked in the windows. Everything was as they'd left it yesterday.

He circled the entire house but found no evidence that anyone was there now or had been there since they'd evacuated.

He dug Nina's spare key from the dirt in the flowerpot on the porch and opened the door, his weapon still ready.

He didn't need it. The B and B was empty. Kip hadn't taken Nina here. He didn't plan to haul her away on a boat. Sinking to the arm of the love seat, Jase massaged his temples. Could it really be as simple as waiting and watching at the wharf?

It might not be that simple. Kip could be in disguise. He could conceal Nina in a trunk. His gut rolled again, but it had nothing to do with the poison that had already left his system.

What resources did Kip have on the island? He knew nobody. The police considered him a person of interest. He'd been posing as a drunk his entire time on the island, hanging out with Lou, telling her tall tales about helicopters.

His pulse leaped. Kip hadn't told Lou about the helicopter. She'd overheard him on the phone asking about a helipad on the island. Maybe Lou's habit of eavesdropping got her killed.

He rushed to the window and looked at the sky over the sound. He'd seen an orange rescue helicopter over the bay before. There had to be a helipad on the island.

And Kip had been inquiring about one because he planned to leave the island by helicopter—with Nina.

He holstered his gun and waded into the yard. The force of the water had knocked down the fence he'd been working on for Nina. That could be fixed, but once Nina boarded that helicopter and left Break Island, she'd be in Tempest's clutches—and that couldn't be fixed.

Jase didn't have time to slog through two feet of water all the way back to town. He made his way to the shed on the other side of the B and B, where Nina kept a rowboat. That was the only way anyone was going to be maneuvering the streets for the next few days.

The water made it impossible for him to open the door of the shed, so he grabbed the ax he'd been using the day before and hacked through the wooden door. The water rushed into the shed and he followed it.

The boat was hanging from two hooks and he lifted it

down and plopped it on top of the water. He unhooked two oars from the inside of the boat and floated out of the shed.

Rowing back to town went a lot faster than wading, but the light of another gloomy day had started to seep through the clouds. The streets were still deserted, although he spotted a rescue vehicle, its orange light revolving on its roof.

He rowed toward the vehicle. County workers were in the back of the truck, tossing sandbags over the side.

Jase yelled to them, "Hey, do you know where there's a helipad on the island?"

They shrugged and shook their heads, but one guy pointed across the street. "Jeff probably knows."

Digging his oars into the water, Jase maneuvered toward Jeff, who was knocking on the door of a business.

"Are you Jeff?"

The man turned around. "What are you doing out here?"

"I'm trying to find someone. The guys back there said you might know where a helipad is on the island."

"Sure I do, but I hope you're not thinking of taking a helicopter off the island. Even though the tail end of this storm is riding through, the air is still unstable."

"No, no, I'm not, but that's where my friend is."

"The only helipad I know about is on top of one of the old warehouse buildings at the end of the pier at the town wharf. It's past Ned's Bait Shop. You can't miss it. The other warehouses have peaked roofs and this one's is flat and higher than the rest."

"Thanks." Jase had never rowed as a sport, but if he had, this stint would win him a gold medal.

By the time he hit the pier, he didn't need the boat anymore. The water here had already receded, although it had left many of the boats in the slips at odd angles or lodged on top of the gangplanks beside the slips.

He stashed the boat by the bait shop and rounded the corner of a tall abandoned building behind it. When he looked toward the end of the pier and the warehouses huddled there, his heart stammered in his chest.

A yellow Bell helicopter was stationed on top of the last warehouse, its blades already spinning.

Of course, Kip would want an early start before boat and foot traffic swarmed the wharf.

Jase dropped his backpack and sloughed off his jacket. Clutching his Glock pistol, he ran toward the warehouses. She hadn't left yet. She hadn't left yet.

People emerged onto the roof and Jase dived against the side of the first warehouse. He had to maintain the element of surprise.

He darted to the next warehouse, looking skyward. He caught a glimpse of three people on the roof—Nina was one of them. So, Kip had help.

He launched himself at the fourth and final warehouse. When he reached the door, he found it locked with a brand-new padlock. With the butt of his gun, he broke off the lock and burst into the warehouse.

Kip hadn't left any backup personnel, but what he saw on the floor of the warehouse made his jaw drop—a bed, food, all the comforts of home. At least Kip hadn't hung Nina from the ceiling by her wrists, but the fact that he'd taken such good care of her scared the hell out of him.

The thwacking of the blades on the roof grew louder. He knew that sound—liftoff.

A set of stairs led to the roof, and Jase took them two at a time. He thrust the heels of his hands against the board covering the opening to the roof and scrambled through it, landing on his hands and knees in a puddle of water.

Nina was already in the chopper, and her eyes widened as she spotted him. Kip had one foot on the step and one on the roof.

Jase shot him.

Kip spun around and his dirty-blond hair fell over his eyes, making him look like the old Kip. He clawed at his waistband, most likely reaching for his weapon.

But the chopper pilot must've had his own orders because he lifted off the roof of the warehouse.

Jase heard Nina's scream merge with the whine of the helicopter as it took off, Kip dangling from the doorway.

She couldn't go any farther or higher or she'd be lost to him forever. He waved his hands over his head and yelled, "Jump! Jump over the water!"

Would she do it? Could he even ask her to? She could lose her baby, but if she went with Tempest, she would lose him anyway.

Jase waved his arms again and pointed down. Would she understand? Did she know what she had to do?

The helicopter lurched over the water, weighed down by Kip hanging on to the stands. It hadn't gained much height yet.

She had to do it. Now.

As the chopper cleared the boats, Nina stepped over Kip, hugged herself and dropped into thin air.

Epilogue

Her eyes flew open and she convulsively clutched at the white sheets. A large, warm hand covered one of hers and she looked into the dark chocolate eyes of her baby's new father.

Jase brought her hand to his lips and pressed them against her palm. "Did you have another nightmare?"

"It wasn't so bad this time. I was falling out of a plane, but I landed on a puffy white cloud."

"That's a lot better than landing in a freezing-cold, choppy bay."

"Not something I want to repeat anytime soon."

"Not many people could've done it." He threaded his fingers through hers. "You were incredibly brave."

"I'm not so sure about that, given the alternative. The prospect of becoming a breeder for Tempest was not something I was relishing." She shivered despite the warmth of the room and Jase's touch. "How did they think they could get away with that?"

"They almost did." He chafed her hand between his. "Tempest's leader calls himself Caliban, and he's certifiable. We have a dire situation on our hands."

"Do you know… Did they ever find Kip's body?"

"Yes. Technically, he drowned."

"Who was he?"

He lifted a shoulder. "A Tempest agent we haven't identified yet."

"He killed Lou and Chris." Her bottom lip quivered. "They must've found out something about him that night they were all together."

"Kip's not the kind of guy to leave loose ends."

She smoothed the sheet over her belly and pressed her hand against her burgeoning bump. Holding her breath, she waited to feel some movement, some sign that Will was okay, not that she'd been feeling him move before her jump into the bay.

Jase traced her hand. "He's going to be okay."

"I'm scared."

"I know. Me, too."

"Are we ready to see what's what?" Dr. Day bustled into the room followed by a nurse with a cart.

"I don't feel any movement."

"You're not quite five months, so that's not so unusual. Everything looks good from the outside. Now let's see about the inside." Dr. Day folded the sheet down and lifted Nina's top to expose her abdomen.

She snapped on a pair of gloves, flicked on the ultrasound and held up a tube of jelly. "This is going to be a little cold and I know you're trying to stay warm, so I apologize in advance."

As the doctor spread the jelly over her bump, Jase squeezed her hand.

Dr. Day applied the paddle and circled her belly. "Ah, there he is."

Nina's head had rolled to the side and she was staring at the image so hard her eyes burned. "Is he okay? Can you tell? Is he moving?"

"Looks fine to me." She winked at Jase. "Do you want to hear the heartbeat, Dad?"

"He's not…" Nina's eyes flew to Jase's face, but he just grinned.

"Of course I want to hear his heartbeat."

The *thump, thump* echoed in Nina's own heart and her eyes brimmed with tears. "He's okay."

"I told you he would be." Jase leaned over and kissed her mouth. "A little jump from a chopper isn't enough to deter him. Maybe he'll be a navy SEAL or something."

"Stop." She poked his thigh as a tear trailed from her eye into her ear. "I'm hoping he'll be an accountant."

Dr. Day clicked a button. "I just took his picture." She plucked a few tissues from the box on the tray and wiped the jelly from Nina's abdomen.

"I'll have the nurse bring by the picture." Dr. Day stopped at the door. "I understand you'll be leaving the base here at Kitsap. Just let me know where you wind up so I can send your file on to your next ob-gyn."

Jase cleared his throat. "Doc, that information is classified. We'll be taking Nina's file with us when we leave in a few days."

"Understood, Lieutenant Bennett."

"Haven't heard that in a while."

"Former Lieutenant Bennett." She waved and shut the door behind her.

"You're not even going to tell me where I'm headed, are you?"

He pushed back from his chair and sat on the edge of her bed. "As long as Tempest is out there, you and Will are in danger. Prospero will protect you until it's safe."

"When will that be, Jase? You don't even know who Caliban is. You don't even know his endgame."

"We'll find him, Nina. We'll figure it out."

"You?" She pleated the folds of the sheet. "You, personally?"

"Just like surveillance, hunting down Caliban is not my job, either. I thought I told you what my job was."

"Personal security?"

"Otherwise known as babysitting."

"And who are you babysitting this time? Some Saudi princess? A sexy German spy?"

He slipped his hands beneath her top and caressed her belly. "Naw, just a crazy pregnant lady."

She grabbed his wrist. "You'll be with me in the secret location?"

"I'm going to be right with you all the way, Nina. I'll even be there in the delivery room and beyond, if you'll have me."

"Oh, I'll have you, Jason Bennett, but we're a package deal."

"I wouldn't have it any other way."

* * * * *

Look for more of Carol Ericson's
BROTHERS IN ARMS: RETRIBUTION
miniseries later in 2015,
wherever Harlequin Intrigue books
and ebooks are sold!

Read on for a sneak peek of
LONE RIDER
The next installment in
THE MONTANA HAMILTONS *series*
from New York Times *bestselling author*
B.J. Daniels.
When danger claims her, rescue comes from the one
man she least expects...

CHAPTER ONE

THE MOMENT JACE CALDER saw his sister's face, he feared the worst. His heart sank. Emily, his troubled little sister, had been doing so well since she'd gotten the job at the Sarah Hamilton Foundation in Big Timber, Montana.

"What's wrong?" he asked as he removed his Stetson, pulled up a chair at the Big Timber Java coffee shop and sat down across from her. Tossing his hat on the seat of an adjacent chair, he braced himself for bad news.

Emily blinked her big blue eyes. Even though she was closing in on twenty-five, he often caught glimpses of the girl she'd been. Her pixie cut, once a dark brown like his own hair, was dyed black. From thirteen on, she'd been piercing anything she could. At sixteen she'd begun getting tattoos and drinking. It wasn't until she'd turned seventeen that she'd run away, taken up with a thirty-year-old biker drug-dealer thief and ended up in jail for the first time.

But while Emily still had the tattoos and the piercings, she'd changed after the birth of her daughter, and after snagging this job with Bo Hamilton.

"What's wrong is Bo," his sister said. Bo had insisted her employees at the foundation call her by her first name. "Pretty cool for a boss, huh?" his sister had said at the time. He'd been surprised. That didn't sound like the woman he knew.

But who knew what was in Bo's head lately. Four

months ago her mother, Sarah, who everyone believed dead the past twenty-two years, had suddenly shown up out of nowhere. According to what he'd read in the papers, Sarah had no memory of the past twenty-two years.

He'd been worried it would hurt the foundation named for her. Not to mention what a shock it must have been for Bo.

Emily leaned toward him and whispered, "Bo's... She's gone."

"Gone?"

"Before she left Friday, she told me that she would be back by ten this morning. She hasn't shown up, and no one knows where she is."

That *did* sound like the Bo Hamilton he knew. The thought of her kicked up that old ache inside him. He'd been glad when Emily had found a job and moved back to town with her baby girl. But he'd often wished her employer had been anyone but Bo Hamilton—the woman he'd once asked to marry him.

He'd spent the past five years avoiding Bo, which wasn't easy in a county as small as Sweet Grass. Crossing paths with her, even after five years, still hurt. It riled him in a way that only made him mad at himself for letting her get to him after all this time.

"What do you mean, *gone*?" he asked now.

Emily looked pained. "I probably shouldn't be telling you this—"

"Em," he said impatiently. She'd been doing so well at this job, and she'd really turned her life around. He couldn't bear the thought that Bo's disappearance might derail her second chance. Em's three-year-old daughter Jodie desperately needed her mom to stay on track.

Leaning closer again, she whispered, "Apparently

there are funds missing from the foundation. An auditor's been going over all the records since Friday."

He sat back in surprise. No matter what he thought of Bo, he'd never imagined this. The woman was already rich. She wouldn't need to divert funds...

"And that's not the worst of it," Emily said. "I was told she's on a camping trip in the mountains."

"So, she isn't really gone."

Em waved a hand. "She took her camping gear, saddled up and left Saturday afternoon. Apparently she's the one who called the auditor, so she knew he would be finished and wanting to talk to her this morning!"

Jace considered this news. If Bo really were on the run with the money, wouldn't she take her passport and her SUV as far as the nearest airport? But why would she run at all? He doubted Bo had ever had a problem that her daddy, the senator, hadn't fixed for her. She'd always had a safety net. Unlike him.

He'd been on his own since eighteen. He'd been a senior in high school, struggling to pay the bills, hang on to the ranch and raise his wild kid sister after his parents had been killed in a small plane crash. He'd managed to save the ranch, but he hadn't been equipped to raise Emily and had made his share of mistakes.

A few months ago, his sister had gotten out of jail and gone to work for Bo. He'd been surprised she'd given Emily a chance. He'd had to readjust his opinion of Bo—but only a little. Now this.

"There has to be an explanation," he said, even though he knew firsthand that Bo often acted impulsively. She did whatever she wanted, damn the world. But now his little sister was part of that world. How could she leave Emily and the rest of the staff at the foundation to face this alone?

"I sure hope everything is all right," his sister said. "Bo is so sweet."

Sweet wasn't a word he would have used to describe her. Sexy in a cowgirl way, yes, since most of the time she dressed in jeans, boots and a Western shirt—all of which accented her very nice curves. Her long, sandy-blond hair was often pulled up in a ponytail or wrestled into a braid that hung over one shoulder. Since her wide green eyes didn't need makeup to give her that girl-next-door look, she seldom wore it.

"I can't believe she wouldn't show up. Something must have happened," Emily said loyally.

He couldn't help being skeptical based on Bo's history. But given Em's concern, he didn't want to add his own kindling to the fire.

"Jace, I just have this bad feeling. You're the best tracker in these parts. I know it's a lot to ask, but would you go find her?"

He almost laughed. Given the bad blood between him and Bo? "I'm the last person—"

"I'm really worried about her. I know she wouldn't run off."

Jace wished *he* knew that. "Look, if you're really that concerned, maybe you should call the sheriff. He can get search and rescue—"

"No," Emily cried. "No one knows what's going on over at the foundation. We have to keep this quiet. That's why you have to go."

He'd never been able to deny his little sister anything, but this was asking too much.

"Please, Jace."

He swore silently. Maybe he'd get lucky and Bo would return before he even got saddled up. "If you're that worried…" He got to his feet and reached for his hat, telling himself it shouldn't take him long to find Bo if she'd gone up into the Crazies, as the Crazy Mountains were known locally. He'd grown up in those mountains. His father had been an avid hunter who'd taught him everything about mountain survival.

If Bo had gone rogue with the foundation's funds… He hated to think what that would do not only to Emily's job but also to her recovery. She idolized her boss. So did Josie, who was allowed the run of the foundation office.

But finding Bo was one thing. Bringing her back to face the music might be another. He started to say as much to Emily, but she cut him off.

"Oh, Jace, thank you so much. If anyone can find her, it's you."

He smiled at his sister as he set his Stetson firmly on his head and made her a promise. "I'll find Bo Hamilton and bring her back." One way or the other.

CHAPTER TWO

Bo HAMILTON ROSE with the sun, packed up camp and saddled up as a squirrel chattered at her from a nearby pine tree. Overhead, high in the Crazy Mountains, Montana's big, cloudless early summer sky had turned a brilliant blue. The day was already warm. Before she'd left, she'd heard a storm was coming in, but she'd known she'd be out of the mountains long before it hit.

She'd had a devil of a time getting to sleep last night, and after tossing and turning for hours in her sleeping bag, she had finally fallen into a death-like sleep.

But this morning, she'd awakened ready to face whatever would be awaiting her tomorrow back at the office in town. Coming up here in the mountains had been the best thing she could have done. For months she'd been worried and confused as small amounts of money kept disappearing from the foundation.

Then last week, she'd realized that more than a hundred thousand dollars was gone. She'd been so shocked that she hadn't been able to breathe, let alone think. That's when she'd called in an independent auditor. She just hoped she could find out what had happened to the money before anyone got wind of it—especially her father, Senator Buckmaster Hamilton.

Her stomach roiled at the thought. He'd always been

so proud of her for taking over the reins of the foundation that bore her mother's name. All her father needed was another scandal. He was running for the presidency of the United States, something he'd dreamed of for years. Now his daughter was about to go to jail for embezzlement. She could only imagine his disappointment in her—not to mention what it might do to the foundation.

She loved the work the foundation did, helping small businesses in their community. Her father had been worried that she couldn't handle the responsibility. She'd been determined to show him he was wrong. And show herself as well. She'd grown up a lot in the past five years, and running the foundation had given her a sense of purpose she'd badly needed.

That's why she was anxious to find out the results of the audit now that her head was clear. The mountains always did that for her. Breathing in the fresh air now, she swung up in the saddle, spurred her horse and headed down the trail toward the ranch. She'd camped only a couple of hours back into the mountain, so she still had plenty of time, she thought as she rode. The last thing she wanted was to be late to meet with the auditor.

She'd known for some time that there were... *discrepancies* in foundation funds. A part of her had hoped that it was merely a mistake—that someone would realize he or she had made an error—so she wouldn't have to confront anyone about the slip.

Bo knew how naive that was, but she couldn't bear to think that one of her employees was behind the theft. Yes, her employees were a ragtag bunch. There was Albert Drum, a seventy-two-year-young former banker who worked with the recipients of the foundation loans. Emily Calder, twenty-four, took care of the website, research, communication and marketing. The only other employee was forty-eight-year-old widow Norma Branstetter, who was in charge of fund-raising.

Employees and board members reviewed the applications that came in for financial help. But Bo was the one responsible for the money that came and went through the foundation.

Unfortunately, she trusted her employees so much that she often let them run the place, including dealing with the financial end of things. She hadn't been paying close enough attention. How else could there be unexplained expenditures?

Her father had warned her about the people she hired, saying she had to be careful. But she loved giving jobs to those who desperately needed another chance. Her employees had become a second family to her.

Just the thought that one of her employees might be responsible made her sick to her stomach. True, she was a sucker for a hard-luck story. But she trusted the people she'd hired. The thought brought tears to her eyes. They all tried so hard and were so appreciative of their jobs. She refused to believe any one of them would steal from the foundation.

So what had happened to the missing funds?

She hadn't ridden far when her horse nickered and raised his head as if sniffing the wind. Spurring him forward, she continued through the dense trees. The pine boughs sighed in the breeze, releasing the smells of early summer in the mountains she'd grown up with. She loved the Crazy Mountains. She loved them especially at this time of year. They rose from the valley into high snow-capped peaks, the awe-inspiring range running for miles to the north like a mountainous island in a sea of grassy plains.

What she appreciated most about the Crazies was that

a person could get lost in them, she thought. A hunter had done just that last year.

She'd ridden down the ridge some distance, the sun moving across the sky over her head, before she caught the strong smell of smoke. This morning she'd put her campfire out using the creek water nearby. Too much of Montana burned every summer because of lightning storms and careless people, so she'd made sure her fire was extinguished before she'd left.

Now reining in, she spotted the source of the smoke. A small campfire burned below her in the dense trees of a protected gully. She stared down into the camp as smoke curled up. While it wasn't that unusual to stumble across a backpacker this deep in the Crazies, it *was* strange for a camp to be so far off the trail. Also, she didn't see anyone below her on the mountain near the fire. Had whoever camped there failed to put out the fire before leaving?

Bo hesitated, feeling torn because she didn't want to take the time to ride all the way down the mountain to the out-of-the-way camp. Nor did she want to ride into anyone's camp unless necessary.

But if the camper had failed to put out the fire, that was another story.

"Hello?" she called down the mountainside.

A hawk let out a cry overhead, momentarily startling her.

"Hello?" she called again, louder.

No answer. No sign of anyone in the camp.

Bo let out an aggravated sigh and spurred her horse. She had a long ride back and didn't need a detour. But she still had plenty of time if she hurried. As she made her way down into the ravine, she caught glimpses of the camp and the smoking campfire, but nothing else.

The hidden-away camp finally came into view below

her. She could see that whoever had camped there hadn't made any effort at all to put out the fire. She looked for horseshoe tracks but saw only boot prints in the dust that led down to the camp.

A quiet seemed to fall over the mountainside. No hawk called out again from high above the trees. No squirrel chattered at her from a pine bough. Even the breeze seemed to have gone silent.

Bo felt a sudden chill as if the sun had gone down—an instant before the man appeared so suddenly from out of the dense darkness of the trees. He grabbed her, yanked her down from the saddle and clamped an arm around her as he shoved the dirty blade of a knife in her face.

"Well, look at you," he said hoarsely against her ear. "Ain't you a sight for sore eyes? Guess it's my lucky day."

JACE HAD JUST knocked at the door when another truck drove up from the direction of the corrals. As Senator Buckmaster Hamilton himself opened the door, he was looking past Jace's shoulder. Jace glanced back to see Cooper Barnett climb out of his truck and walk toward them.

Jace turned back around. "I'm Jace Calder," he said, holding out his hand as the senator's gaze shifted to him.

The senator frowned but shook his hand. "I know who you are. I'm just wondering what's got you on my doorstep so early in the morning."

"I'm here about your daughter Bo."

Buckmaster looked to Cooper. "Tell me you aren't here about my daughter Olivia."

Cooper laughed. "My pregnant bride is just fine, thanks."

The senator let out an exaggerated breath and turned his attention back to Jace. "What's this about—?" But before he could finish, a tall, elegant blonde woman appeared at his side. Jace recognized Angelina Broadwater Hamilton, the senator's second wife. The rumors about her being kicked out of the house to make way for Buckmaster's first wife weren't true, it seemed.

She put a hand on Buckmaster's arm. "It's the auditor calling from the foundation office. He's looking for Bo. She didn't show up for work today, and there seems to be a problem."

"That's why I'm here," Jace said.

"Me too," Cooper said, sounding surprised.

"Come in, then," Buckmaster said, waving both men inside. Once he'd closed the big door behind them, he asked, "Now what's this about Bo?"

"I was just talking to one of the wranglers," Cooper said, jumping in ahead of Jace. "Bo apparently left Saturday afternoon on horseback, saying she'd be back this morning, but she hasn't returned."

"That's what I heard as well," Jace said, taking the opening. "I need to know where she might have gone."

Both Buckmaster and Cooper looked to him. "You sound as if you're planning to go after her," the senator said.

"I am."

"Why would you do that? I didn't think you two were seeing each other?" Cooper asked like the protective brother-in-law he was.

"We're not," Jace said.

"Wait a minute," the senator said. "You're the one who stood her up for the senior prom. I'll never forget it. My baby cried for weeks."

Jace nodded. "That would be me."

"But you've dated Bo more recently than senior prom," Buckmaster was saying.

"Five years ago," he said. "But that doesn't have anything to do with this. I have my reasons for wanting to see Bo come back. My sister works at the foundation."

"Why wouldn't Bo come back?" the senator demanded.

Behind him, Angelina made a disparaging sound. "Because there's money missing from the foundation along with your daughter." She looked at Jace. "You said your sister works down there?"

He smiled, seeing that she was clearly judgmental of the "kind of people" Bo had hired to work at the foundation. "My sister doesn't have access to any of the money, if that's what you're worried about." He turned to the senator again. "The auditor is down at the foundation office, trying to sort it out. Bo needs to be there. I thought you might have some idea where she might have gone in the mountains. I thought I'd go find her."

The senator looked to his son-in-law. Cooper shrugged.

"Cooper, you were told she planned to be back Sunday?" her father said. "She probably changed her mind or went too far, not realizing how long it would take her to get back. If she had an appointment today with an auditor, I'm sure she's on her way as we speak."

"Or she's hiding up there and doesn't want to be found," Angelina quipped from the couch. "If she took that money, she could be miles from here by now." She groaned. "It's always something with your girls, isn't it?"

"I highly doubt Bo has taken off with any foundation money," the senator said and shot his wife a disgruntled look. "Every minor problem isn't a major scandal," he said and sighed, clearly irritated with his wife.

When he and Bo had dated, she'd told him that her stepmother was always quick to blame her and her sisters no matter the situation. As far as Jace could tell, there was no love lost on either side.

"Maybe we should call the sheriff," Cooper said.

Angelina let out a cry. "That's all we need—more negative publicity. It will be bad enough when this gets out. But if search and rescue is called in and the sheriff has to go up there... For all we know, Bo could be meeting someone in those mountains."

Jace hadn't considered she might have an accomplice. "That's why I'm the best person to go after her."

"How do you figure that?" Cooper demanded, giving him a hard look.

"She already doesn't like me, and the feeling is mutual. Maybe you're right and she's hightailing it home as we speak," Jace said. "But whatever's going on with her, I'm going to find her and make sure she gets back."

"You sound pretty confident of that," the senator said sounding almost amused.

"I know these mountains, and I'm not a bad tracker. I'll find her. But that's big country. My search would go faster if I have some idea where she was headed when she left."

"There's a trail to the west of the ranch that connects with the Sweet Grass Creek trail," her father said.

Jace rubbed a hand over his jaw. "That trail forks not far up."

"She usually goes to the first camping spot before the fork," the senator said. "It's only a couple of hours back in. I'm sure she wouldn't go any farther than that. It's along Loco Creek."

"I know that spot," Jace said.

Cooper looked to his father-in-law. "You want me to get some men together and go search for her? That makes more sense than sending—"

Buckmaster shook his head and turned to Jace. "I remember your father. The two of you were volunteers on a search years ago. I was impressed with both of you. I'm putting my money on you finding her if she doesn't turn up on her own. I'll give you 'til sundown."

"Make it twenty-four hours. There's a storm coming so I plan to be back before it hits. If we're both not back by then, send in the cavalry," he said and with a tip of his hat, headed for the door.

Behind him, he heard Cooper say, "Sending him could be a mistake."

"The cowboy's mistake," Buckmaster said. "I know my daughter. She's on her way back, and she isn't going to like that young man tracking her down. Jace Calder is the one she almost married."

* * * * *

Find out what happens next in
LONE RIDER
by New York Times
bestselling author B.J. Daniels
available August 2015,
wherever HQN Books and ebooks are sold.
www.Harlequin.com

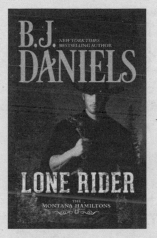

COMING NEXT MONTH FROM

 HARLEQUIN®

INTRIGUE

Available August 18, 2015

#1587 SWITCHBACK
by Catherine Anderson
A reader favorite! PI Bud Mac Phearson and single mother Mallory Christiani race against time to rescue her daughter. Mac will give anything to ensure a happy ending for Mallory and her child—even his own life.

#1588 SUSPICIONS
The Battling McGuire Boys • by Cynthia Eden
Years ago, Mark Montgomery saved Ava McGuire from a night of terror. But when a killer comes hunting again, and passion draws them closer, will Mark's secrets be their downfall?

#1589 McCULLEN'S SECRET SON
The Heroes of Horseshoe Creek • by Rita Herron
When her husband's killers kidnap her son, Willow James Howard accepts help from rodeo star Brett McCullen, the man who broke her heart. With the ransom deadline looming, Brett must fight to save the family he never knew he wanted...

#1590 BLACK CANYON CONSPIRACY
The Ranger Brigade • by Cindi Myers
Former Special Forces soldier Marco Cruz saved TV reporter Lauren Starling from a hostage ordeal. Now someone wants her dead—and the handsome Ranger wants to be the one to protect her...

#1591 TEXAS PREY
Mason Ridge • by Barb Han
Abducted years ago, Rebecca Hughes needs rancher Brody Fields to bring the kidnapper to justice. As they uncover answers to difficult—and deadly—questions, can Brody trust the woman who once shattered his heart?

#1592 AGENT TO THE RESCUE
Special Agents at the Altar • by Lisa Childs
When FBI special agent Dalton Reyes discovers an amnesiac injured bride, his protective instincts kick in. As Elizabeth Schroeder faces her dark past, Dalton must keep her and her adopted daughter safe from the forces determined to reclaim them.

SPECIAL EXCERPT FROM

H **HARLEQUIN**

INTRIGUE

Read on for a sneak preview of
SUSPICIONS, the next installment in
THE BATTLING McGUIRE BOYS
by New York Times *bestselling author*
Cynthia Eden

Years ago, Mark Montgomery saved Ava McGuire from
a night of terror. But when a killer comes hunting again,
and passion draws them closer, will Mark's secrets be
their downfall?

Ava McGuire didn't have a lot of safe havens. And, outside of her family, there weren't exactly a lot of people she trusted.

In fact, only one person came to mind…

Mark Montgomery.

Ava slammed her car door and turned to the house. It was the middle of the night. *Not* the right time to be paying a visit to Mark's ranch, but she wasn't exactly overwhelmed with options.

I need to see him.

She straightened her shoulders and she marched toward his front door. She didn't let the memories swamp her as she climbed up the steps of the big, wraparound porch. If she thought too much about the past, it would hurt. Those memories always did.

So she shoved the thoughts into the recesses of her mind, and she climbed those front steps. She reached for the doorbell, but then the door opened.

HIEXP0815

Mark was there.

Tall, handsome, strong—*Mark*. His blond hair was tousled, and the light shone behind him, glinting off his shoulders. Very broad and bare shoulders because he wasn't wearing a shirt. Just a pair of low-slung jeans.

"Ava?" He reached out to her. "What are you doing here?"

I needed to see you. I had to talk with someone…with someone who wouldn't think I was crazy.

Those words wanted to tumble out of her mouth, but she was trying to play things cool and not come across as the insane one. At least, not right away. She knew there were plenty of folks who already thought she was nuts or, much worse, a cold-blooded killer.

The rumors about her had persisted for years.

But…Mark had never seemed to believe those stories. He'd always stood by Ava and her family.

"I need your help," she told him quietly. She looked over his shoulder, hoping that no one else was there. The ranch house was huge, sprawling, but normally his staff stayed in separate quarters. She really didn't want anyone to overhear the confession she was about to make.

He pulled her into the house and shut the door behind her. "Ava, I'll give you anything you need."

Don't miss
SUSPICIONS by Cynthia Eden,
available September 2015 wherever
Harlequin Intrigue® books and ebooks are sold.

www.Harlequin.com